IRELAND

GOOD STORIES REVEAL as much, or more, about a locale as any map or guidebook. Whereabouts Press is dedicated to publishing books that will enlighten a traveler to the soul of a place. By bringing a country's stories to the English-speaking reader, we hope to convey its culture through literature. Books from Whereabouts Press are essential companions for the curious traveler, and for the person who appreciates how fine writing enhances one's experiences in the world.

"Coming newly into Spanish, I lacked two essentials—a childhood in the language, which I could never acquire, and a sense of its literature, which I could."

—Alastair Reid, *Whereabouts: Notes on Being a Foreigner*

OTHER TRAVELER'S LITERARY COMPANIONS

Amsterdam edited by Manfred Wolf

Australia edited by Robert Ross

Chile edited by Katherine Silver

Costa Rica edited by Barbara Ras
with a foreword by Oscar Arias

Cuba edited by Ann Louise Bardach

Greece edited by Artemis Leontis

Israel edited by Michael Gluzman and Naomi Seidman
with a foreword by Robert Alter

Italy edited by and translated by Lawrence Venuti

Japan edited by Jeffrey Angles and J. Thomas Rimer

Mexico edited by C. M. Mayo

Prague edited by Paul Wilson

Spain edited by Peter Bush and Lisa Dillman

Vietnam edited by John Balaban
and Nguyen Qui Duc

IRELAND

A TRAVELER'S LITERARY COMPANION

EDITED BY

JAMES MC ELROY

WHEREABOUTS PRESS
BERKELEY, CALIFORNIA

Published by
Whereabouts Press
Berkeley, California
www.whereaboutspress.com

Distributed to the trade by PGW / Perseus Distribution.

Map of Ireland by BookMatters

MANUFACTURED IN THE UNITED STATES OF AMERICA

Library of Congress Cataloging-in-Publication Data

Ireland / edited by James Mc Elroy.
Ireland : a traveler's literary companion /
edited by James Mc Elroy.
p.   cm.—(A traveler's literary companion ; 14)
ISBN-13: 978-1-883513-17-7 (alk. paper)
ISBN-10: 1-883513-17-0 (alk. paper)
1. Short stories, English.
2. English fiction—Irish authors.
3. English fiction—20th century.
4. Ireland—Fiction.
I. McElroy, James.
PR8876.I7   2007
823'.010832415—dc22   2007027349

5 4 3 2 1

Contents

Preface   ix

LEINSTER

James Joyce   *Ulysses*   1
Elizabeth Cullinan   *A Good Loser*   11
Hugo Hamilton   *The Homesick Industry*   39
Éilís Ní Dhuibhne   *A Visit to Newgrange*   47

MUNSTER

Frank O'Connor   *The American Wife*   59
Seán Mac Mathúna   *The Man Who Stepped
   on His Soul*   77
Edna O'Brien   *A Scandalous Woman*   95

CONNAUGHT

J. M. Synge   *The Aran Islands*   131
Desmond Hogan   *The Last Time*   147
Brian Moore   *Going Home*   156
Ita Daly   *The Lady with the Red Shoes*   162
John McGahern   *The Stoat*   178

ULSTER

Brian Friel   *The Saucer of Larks*   187
Gerry Adams   *The Mountains of Mourne*   198
Patrick Kavanagh   *A Visit to Dublin*   223

Permissions   237
About the Editor   239

Preface

Ireland: A Traveler's Literary Companion features some of the Emerald Isle's most intriguing—and exquisite—writers. The first of these is James Joyce whose masterpiece, *Ulysses*, set the stage for world literature in the twentieth century. To give readers an immediate sense of just how assiduous Joyce is when it comes to epiphanizing the written word, this collection begins with the opening scene from *Ulysses*—a disarming narrative that provides a subtle measure of Dublin's culture wars from inside a superannuated Martello Tower (the tower in question now serves as Ireland's Joyce Museum) near Dún Laoghaire on the south side of Dublin Bay.

Close on the heels of *Ulysses*, the other pieces that make up the first section of this literary companion (the book's four sections are named after the Four Provinces of Ireland) introduce readers to the agonies and ecstasies of life in the New Ireland. The first of these is a wonderful and engaging short by Irish-American writer, Elizabeth Cullinan, who—in "A Good Loser"—describes the existential realities of life, love, happiness (and unhappiness) in modern Dublin. Cullinan is followed by Hugo Hamilton who explores what it feels like to be part of the Irish tourist trade, or, to be more specific, someone who dabbles in

Aran sweaters. The last piece in this section—the Leinster section—is Éilís Ní Dhuibhne's "A Visit to Newgrange," a story that examines the vicissitudes of modern life in Dublin while taking the reader on a brief excursion, outside Dublin, to one of Ireland's premier tourist sites: the Megalithic Tomb at Newgrange in County Meath.

The next section of *Ireland: A Traveler's Literary Companion*—the Munster section—takes its cue from Frank O'Connor, one of Ireland's most renowned short story writers, who, in "The American Wife," delivers a commentary on family life in Cork and family values in the United States. From Cork we then head west to Kerry where Seán Mac Mathúna, with "The Man Who Stepped on His Soul," introduces us to the windswept aesthetic of the Banna Strand and a lone (lost) figure in the shape of Brother Tom Mullins, a self-proclaimed "geographer." Then there is Edna O'Brien who introduces us to the ways of County Clare with one of her most mesmerizing works in the guise of "A Scandalous Woman." O'Brien, a prolific novelist who acquired an international reputation with the publication of her first novel, *The Country Girls* (1960), provides, in this extended tale, a real tour de force; a provocative look at sexual mores and sexual miscommunication in the Ireland of yesteryear.

After the mastery that is "The Scandalous Woman," the third section of this book—the Connaught section— shifts gears and brings us out to the Aran Islands off the Galway/Clare Coast. Populated by Irish speakers, the Aran Islands remain one of Ireland's most evocative tourist destinations with ferries servicing all three islands (Inis Mór, Inis Meáin, Inis Óirr) on a regular basis. As a brief but enchanting introduction to the islands, J.M. Synge's memoir of his experiences on the islands beginning in 1898 (his finished work, *The Aran Islands*, was not published until 1907) takes us right inside a world of ancient customs and uncommon decencies.

In marked contrast to Synge's account of the Arans, Desmond Hogan brings us back to the mainland with a moving rendition of young love in Galway entitled, "The Last Time." Next on our list of contributors is Brian Moore who, so often praised for his concise but penetrating novels about life in Belfast—*The Lonely Passion of Judith Hearne* and *The Feast of Lupercal*—manages, in "Going Home" (the last thing Moore wrote before he died in 1999), to produce a close meditation on a headstone inscription he comes across somewhere in Connemara. With "The Lady with the Red Shoes" Ita Daly continues our journey through Connaught by taking us to the McAndrews Hotel in County Mayo where she ponders the mysteries of common speech and what used to be called "the curse of emigration." John McGahern, surely one of Ireland's greatest writers since Joyce, wraps up our tour of Connaught with "The Stoat," a piece that renders a powerful analogue between people and lesser (?) mammals at a hotel near Strandhill, County Sligo.

The fourth and final section of this collection—the Ulster section—features some stories set in Ireland's most northern province. These stories call on readers to explore a region which, because of The Troubles, has seen far fewer visitors (and this is especially true of Northern Ireland's six counties) than has been the case anywhere else in Ireland. All of which is a real shame once we stop to consider the obvious: Northern Ireland harbors some of Ireland's most exquisite natural beauties and bustling social centers— The Glens of Antrim, The Giant's Causeway, Fair Head, Rathlin Island, The Mountains of Mourne, and, as it was once called, "The Athens of the North": Belfast.

The writers who made the final cut (as per Ulster and all that) include Brian Friel—most famous for *Dancing at Lughnasa*—with "The Saucer of Larks" as set in County Donegal. From Donegal we then shoot down to Belfast and take in some sectarian banter thanks to Gerry Adams who shows himself (as well as being longstanding spokesman for Sinn Féin) to be an accomplished author in his own right: something he proves in "The Mountains of Mourne" where he travels between the Catholic-Protestant backstreets of Belfast and the Silent Valley of the Mourne Mountains in County Down. The very last entry in *Ireland: A Traveler's Literary Companion* brings us full circle as Patrick Kavanagh, perhaps Ireland's most beloved autodidact and poet, makes a trek from his native Inniskeen, in County Monaghan, all the way down to Dublin and back. As it turns out, "A Visit to Dublin" gives us one last glimpse of Dublin and surrounding counties by re-casting, in a new and visitant light, the old stomping grounds of writers like James Joyce and Oliver St John Gogarty (alias Buck Mulligan of *Ulysses*) long before Ireland ever became known as the Celtic Tiger.

James Mc Elroy
September 2007

Ulysses

James Joyce

STATELY, PLUMP Buck Mulligan came from the stair-head, bearing a bowl of lather on which a mirror and a razor lay crossed. A yellow dressing gown, ungirdled, was sustained gently behind him by the mild morning air. He held the bowl aloft and intoned:

—*Introibo ad altare Dei.*

Halted, he peered down the dark winding stairs and called up coarsely:

—Come up, Kinch. Come up, you fearful Jesuit.

Solemnly he came forward and mounted the round gunrest. He faced about and blessed gravely thrice the tower, the surrounding country and the awaking moun-

JAMES JOYCE (1882–1941) was born in Dublin and is perhaps the most famous prose stylist of the twentieth century. After the publication of *Dubliners* in 1914, Joyce began to use more experimental narratives in his novel, *A Portrait of the Artist as a Young Man* (1916). His even more experimental work *Ulysses* (1922) took some seven years to write and put in motion a radical use of interior monologue. His last work, *Finnegans Wake*, took sixteen years to write and, since its publication in 1939, has both bewitched and bewildered some of the world's leading scholars.

tains. Then, catching sight of Stephen Dedalus, he bent towards him and made rapid crosses in the air, gurgling in his throat and shaking his head. Stephen Dedalus, displeased and sleepy, leaned his arms on the top of the staircase and looked coldly at the shaking gurgling face that blessed him, equine in its length, and at the light untonsured hair, grained and hued like pale oak.

Buck Mulligan peeped an instant under the mirror and then covered the bowl smartly.

—Back to barracks, he said sternly.

He added in a preacher's tone:

—For this, O dearly beloved, is the genuine Christine: body and soul and blood and ouns. Slow music, please. Shut your eyes, gents. One moment. A little trouble about those white corpuscles. Silence, all.

He peered sideways up and gave a long low whistle of call then paused awhile in rapt attention, his even white teeth glistening here and there with gold points. Chrysostomos. Two strong shrill whistles answered through the calm.

—Thanks, old chap, he cried briskly. That will do nicely. Switch off the current, will you?

He skipped off the gunrest and looked gravely at his watcher, gathering about his legs the loose folds of his gown. The plump shadowed face and sullen oval jowl recalled a prelate, patron of arts in the middle ages. A pleasant smile broke quietly over his lips.

—The mockery of it, he said gaily. Your absurd name, an ancient Greek.

He pointed his finger in friendly jest and went over to the parapet, laughing to himself. Stephen Dedalus stepped up, followed him wearily halfway and sat down on the edge of the gunrest, watching him still as he propped his mirror on the parapet, dipped the brush in the bowl and lathered cheeks and neck.

Buck Mulligan's gay voice went on.

—My name is absurd too: Malachi Mulligan, two dactyls. But it has a Hellenic ring, hasn't it? Tripping and sunny like the buck himself. We must go to Athens. Will you come if I can get the aunt to fork out twenty quid?

He laid the brush aside and, laughing with delight, cried:

—Will he come? The jejune jesuit.

Ceasing, he began to shave with care.

—Tell me, Mulligan, Stephen said quietly.

—Yes, my love?

—How long is Haines going to stay in this tower?

Buck Mulligan showed a shaven cheek over his right shoulder.

—God, isn't he dreadful? he said frankly. A ponderous Saxon. He thinks you're not a gentleman. God, these bloody English. Bursting with money and indigestion. Because he comes from Oxford. You know, Dedalus, you have the real Oxford manner. He can't make you out. O, my name for you is the best: Kinch, the knife blade.

He shaved warily over his chin.

—He was raving all night about a black panther, Stephen said. Where is his guncase?

—A woful lunatic, Mulligan said. Were you in a funk?

—I was, Stephen said with energy and growing fear. Out here in the dark with a man I don't know raving and moaning to himself about shooting a black panther. You saved men from drowning. I'm not a hero, however. If he stays on here I am off.

Buck Mulligan frowned at the lather on his razorblade. He hopped down from his perch and began to search his trouser pockets hastily.

—Scutter, he cried thickly.

He came over to the gunrest and, thrusting a hand into Stephen's upper pocket, said:

—Lend us a loan of your noserag to wipe my razor.

Stephen suffered him to pull out and hold up on show by its corner a dirty crumpled handkerchief. Buck Mulligan wiped the razorblade neatly. Then, gazing over the handkerchief, he said:

—The bard's noserag. A new art color for our Irish poets: snotgreen. You can almost taste it, can't you?

He mounted to the parapet again and gazed out over Dublin bay, his fair oakpale hair stirring slightly.

—God, he said quietly. Isn't the sea what Algy calls it: a great sweet mother? The snotgreen sea. The scrotum-tightening sea. *Epi oinopa ponton.* Ah, Dedalus, the Greeks. I must teach you. You must read them in the original. *Thalatta! Thalatta!* She is our great sweet mother. Come and look.

Stephen stood up and went over to the parapet. Leaning on it he looked down on the water and on the mailboat clearing the harbor mouth of Kingstown.

—Our mighty mother, Buck Mulligan said.

He turned abruptly his great searching eyes from the sea to Stephen's face.

—The aunt thinks you killed your mother, he said. That's why she won't let me have anything to do with you.

—Someone killed her, Stephen said gloomily.

—You could have knelt down, damn it, Kinch, when

your dying mother asked you, Buck Mulligan said. I'm hyperborean as much as you. But to think of your mother begging you with her last breath to kneel down and pray for her. And you refused. There is something sinister in you . . .

He broke off and lathered again lightly his farther cheek. A tolerant smile curled his lips.

—But a lovely mummer, he murmured to himself. Kinch, the loveliest mummer of them all.

He shaved evenly and with care, in silence, seriously.

Stephen, an elbow rested on the jagged granite, leaned his palm against his brow and gazed at the fraying edge of his shiny black coat sleeve. Pain, that was not yet the pain of love, fretted his heart. Silently, in a dream she had come to him after her death, her wasted body within its loose brown graveclothes giving off an odor of wax and rosewood, her breath, that had bent upon him, mute, reproachful, a faint odor of wetted ashes. Across the threadbare cuffedge he saw the sea hailed as a great sweet mother by the wellfed voice beside him. The ring of bay and skyline held a dull green mass of liquid. A bowl of white china had stood beside her deathbed holding the green sluggish bile which she had torn up from her rotting liver by fits of loud groaning vomiting.

Buck Mulligan wiped again his razorblade.

—Ah, poor dogsbody, he said in a kind voice. I must give you a shirt and a few noserags. How are the secondhand breeks?

—They fit well enough, Stephen answered.

Buck Mulligan attacked the hollow beneath his underlip.

—The mockery of it, he said contentedly, secondleg

they should be. God knows what poxy bowsy left them off. I have a lovely pair with a hair stripe, grey. You'll look spiffing in them. I'm not joking, Kinch. You look damn well when you're dressed.

—Thanks, Stephen said. I can't wear them if they are grey.

—He can't wear them, Buck Mulligan told his face in the mirror. Etiquette is etiquette. He kills his mother but he can't wear grey trousers.

He folded his razor neatly and with stroking palps of fingers felt the smooth skin.

Stephen turned his gaze from the sea and to the plump face with its smokeblue mobile eyes.

—That fellow I was with in the Ship last night, said Buck Mulligan, says you have g.p.i. He's up in Dottyville with Conolly Norman. General paralysis of the insane.

He swept the mirror a half circle in the air to flash the tidings abroad in sunlight now radiant on the sea. His curling shaven lips laughed and the edges of his white glittering teeth. Laughter seized all his strong wellknit trunk.

—Look at yourself, he said, you dreadful bard.

Stephen bent forward and peered at the mirror held out to him, cleft by a crooked crack, hair on end. As he and others see me. Who chose this face for me? This dogsbody to rid of vermin. It asks me too.

—I pinched it out of the skivvy's room, Buck Mulligan said. It does her all right. The aunt always keeps plain-looking servants for Malachi. Lead him not into temptation. And her name is Ursula.

Laughing again, he brought the mirror away from Stephen's peering eyes.

—The rage of Caliban at not seeing his face in a mirror, he said. If Wilde were only alive to see you.

Drawing back and pointing, Stephen said with bitterness:

—It is a symbol of Irish art. The cracked looking glass of a servant.

Buck Mulligan suddenly linked his arm in Stephen's and walked with him round the tower, his razor and mirror clacking in the pocket where he had thrust them.

—It's not fair to tease you like that, Kinch, is it? he said kindly. God knows you have more spirit than any of them.

Parried again. He fears the lancet of my art as I fear that of his. The cold steel pen.

—Cracked looking glass of a servant. Tell that to the oxy chap downstairs and touch him for a guinea. He's stinking with money and thinks you're not a gentleman. His old fellow made his tin by selling jalap to Zulus or some bloody swindle or other. God, Kinch, if you and I could only work together we might do something for the island. Hellenize it.

Cranly's arm. His arm.

—And to think of your having to beg from these swine. I'm the only one that knows what you are. Why don't you trust me more? What have you up your nose against me? Is it Haines? If he makes any noise here I'll bring down Seymour and we'll give him a ragging worse than they gave Clive Kempthorpe.

Young shouts of moneyed voices in Clive Kempthorpe's rooms. Palefaces: they hold their ribs with laughter, one clasping another, O, I shall expire! Break the news to her gently, Aubrey! I shall die! With slit ribbons of his shirt whipping the air he hops and hobbles round the table, with trousers down at heels, chased by Ades of Magdalen with the tailor's shears. A scared calf's face gilded with marmalade. I don't want to be debagged! Don't you play the giddy ox with me!

Shouts from the open window startling evening in the quadrangle. A deaf gardener, aproned, masked with Matthew Arnold's face, pushes his mower on the somber lawn watching narrowly the dancing motes of grasshalms.

To ourselves . . . new paganism . . . omphalos.

—Let him stay, Stephen said. There's nothing wrong with him except at night.

—Then what is it? Buck Mulligan asked impatiently. Cough it up. I'm quite frank with you. What have you against me now?

They halted, looking towards the blunt cape of Bray Head that lay on the water like the snout of a sleeping whale. Stephen freed his arm quietly.

—Do you wish me to tell you? he asked.

—Yes, what is it? Buck Mulligan answered. I don't remember anything.

He looked in Stephen's face as he spoke. A light wind passed his brow, fanning softly his fair uncombed hair and stirring silver points of anxiety in his eyes.

Stephen, depressed by his own voice, said:

—Do you remember the first day I went to your house after my mother's death?

Buck Mulligan frowned quickly and said:

—What? Where? I can't remember anything. I remember only ideas and sensations. Why? What happened in the name of God?

—You were making tea, Stephen said, and I went across the landing to get more hot water. Your mother and some visitor came out of the drawing room. She asked you who was in your room.

—Yes? Buck Mulligan said. What did I say? I forget.

—You said, Stephen answered, *O, it's only Dedalus whose mother is beastly dead.*

A flush which made him seem younger and more engaging rose to Buck Mulligan's cheek.

—Did I say that? he asked. Well? What harm is that?

He shook his constraint from him nervously.

—And what is death, he asked, your mother's or yours or my own? You saw only your mother die. I see them pop off every day in the Mater and Richmond and cut up into tripes in the dissecting room. It's a beastly thing and nothing else. It simply doesn't matter. You wouldn't kneel down to pray for your mother on her deathbed when she asked you. Why? Because you have the cursed jesuit strain in you, only it's injected the wrong way. To me it's all a mockery and beastly. Her cerebral lobes are not functioning. She calls the doctor Sir Peter Teazle and picks buttercups off the quilt. Humor her till it's over. You crossed her last wish in death and yet you sulk with me because I don't whinge like some hired mute from Lalouette's. Absurd! I suppose I did say it. I didn't mean to offend the memory of your mother.

He had spoken himself into boldness. Stephen, shielding the gaping wounds which the words had left in his heart, said very coldly:

—I am not thinking of the offence to my mother.

—Of what, then? Buck Mulligan asked.

—Of the offence to me, Stephen answered.

Buck Mulligan swung round on his heel.

—O, an impossible person! he exclaimed.

He walked off quickly round the parapet. Stephen stood at his post, gazing over the calm sea towards the headland. Sea and headland now grew dim. Pulses were beating in his eyes, veiling their sight, and he felt the fever of his cheeks.

A voice within the tower called loudly:

—Are you up there, Mulligan?

—I'm coming, Buck Mulligan answered.

He turned towards Stephen and said:

—Look at the sea. What does it care about offences? Chuck Loyola, Kinch, and come on down. The Sassenach wants his morning rashers.

A Good Loser

Elizabeth Cullinan

WHEN I WAS TWENTY-SIX I went to Ireland and lived there for two years. I did this on the strength of a day and a half I'd once spent driving from Cork to Dublin on a three-week vacation in Europe. I was taken with the plain-looking Irish villages, the simple cities, with the modest beauty of the people and the extravagant beauty of the countryside. At home in New York, where I worked for an advertising agency, I began saving money and when I had enough I went back to study at the College of Art in Dublin. Afterwards the time I spent there struck me as the most interesting thing I had to say about myself, and I was always bringing it into the conversation, with the result that eventually I came to disbelieve in those years. I also

ELIZABETH CULLINAN (1933–) was born in New York. An Irish-American, she lived in Ireland for several years in the 1960s. Her short story collections include *The Time of Adam* (1971) and *Yellow Roses* (1977). Novels include such works as *House of Gold* (1969) and *A Change of Scene* (1982). Cullinan has taught at the University of Iowa, the University of Massachusetts, and Fordham University. Awards include a Houghton Mifflin Literary Fellowship and Carnegie Foundation Grant.

became reluctant to go back. From year to year I'd decide I couldn't afford the time or the money to go over for a visit, and the years added up to ten when last summer I was offered the use of a house in Booterstown. A friend of a friend was coming to New York for the month of July. Her name was Hope Hazlitt, and she was a transplanted American such as I'd been, though unlike me she'd taken root. She had some sort of job and she had this house, which she rented furnished and didn't want to leave empty. Hope Hazlitt was also rich, a purebred Presbyterian from Seattle, divorced and with a young son, who was to be enrolled in an American summer camp. I had my doubts about returning under these conspicuously alien auspices, but still, a whole house for a month, rent-free—it seemed too good to pass up. I consulted the map of Dublin that hangs on the wall behind my sofa and located Booterstown on the south side of the city, roughly between Ballsbridge and Blackrock, which meant that it was at least a suburb, not some godforsaken spot, and so I took the plunge.

In a recurrent dream I used to have, pure, classical Dublin had been reconstructed along lines that my sleeping mind must have lifted from forgotten pictures of Mussolini's Italy. All the streets were the width of the New England Thruway, all the buildings were massive blocks of stone, in all the statues the men were musclebound. Dreams have a way of affecting conscious life, and gradually this one took on an authority that I felt less and less able to question, and so I was in a state of joyful relief that day last summer as I rode in from the airport and discovered, street by street, that there were really no changes to speak of. I'd arranged to spend my first night at Buswell's, an inexpensive hotel in the center of town. My room was on the Kildare Street side, and the maid had opened the window to let the place air. I went and looked out. There were gulls roosting on top of the National Museum across the street—I'd forgotten the Dublin gulls. I'd forgotten just how low the Dublin roofscape is, and how low-key the sounds of a business day are in that capital city—how nonchalantly people there go about their business. As I took all this in, the grey city that I'd been carrying around in my head faded into thin air. The real city, incomparably gay and unfathomably careless, was mine once again. I was starting to unpack when the phone rang. It was Hope Hazlitt. She said, "Can you come on out and see the house?" For "on" she said "an," and I was impressed—she still had her American accent, whereas half an hour in Dublin and I was already rushing my words in the Irish way.

I said, "I'm free anytime."

"How about now?" she suggested firmly. "We're leaving first thing in the morning, and I'd like to get things settled."

I said, "Give me an hour or so."

"We'll say half past one." It was then about noon. "You can take the 6, the 7, the 7A, the 8, or the 45 bus. When you get to Booterstown, look on the right-hand side for a big pub called The Punch Bowl. That's the corner of Booterstown Avenue, where you get off. Castle Court is just off Booterstown Avenue."

I'd waited ten years to come back to Dublin and I wasn't going to wait another couple of hours to touch home base. I dashed over to Grafton Street and wandered up and down there in an ecstasy of recognition. I bought an *Irish Times*, I stopped and had bacon and egg at Bewley's; then

I walked down to College Green and caught a No. 6 bus. As I swung on board I had a powerful sense of going away from where I wanted to be, but I was happy, too, riding past the noble Georgian squares, then on into Ballsbridge, where the dark-red brick houses look like small orphanages or reformatories. Ballsbridge is a rich neighborhood; soon it gave way to lesser suburbs. Dublin Bay came into view on the left. Merrion Road expanded to four lanes and became Rock Road. I was unfamiliar with this stretch, and I became distracted and missed the big pub Hope Hazlitt had told me to look out for. By the time I realized my mistake and got off, I was close to Blackrock and I had a long walk back and then another long walk the length of Booterstown Avenue, in both directions, for there was no street marked Castle Court. Not that I minded this walk. Booterstown was everything I could have asked for—a small place, hardly more than one long street lined with grey stone bungalows set close to the curb behind strips of garden where the occasional stunted palm or monkeypuzzle tree grew among purple and pink snapdragons.

Back on Rock Road, I went into The Punch Bowl and asked the barman where Castle Court was. "That's the place off Beech Road," he said, smoothing his hair with one hand and then with the other. "Take the first turn to your right off Booterstown Avenue." He gave me these directions with a look of distrust, which I understood after I'd followed them. Castle Court was a development, a group of twelve identical, brand-new two-story white-washed brick houses that belonged in suburban Long Island or New Jersey. I was bitterly disappointed, half an hour late, angry at having been misdirected, and ready to make light of all this as I rang Hope Hazlitt's doorbell, but Hope wasn't in a light mood. "You're late," she said as she opened the door.

I said, "I got lost. Castle Court isn't marked."

She said, "Yes, it is."

"Not on Booterstown Avenue," I said.

She said, "Come an in." As I stepped inside, two things hit me simultaneously: the house was grotesque, and I was stuck there. "I haven't finished cleaning up yet," said Hope.

"You don't have to bother," I assured her. What I felt was something like "Why waste energy cleaning a place as ugly as this?" But if Hope Hazlitt read my mind or if she noticed the dismay behind my politeness she didn't let on.

"Shall we have a look around?" she said.

What impressed me most about that house was the carpeting, which was mercilessly wall-to-wall—the front hall, the living room, the staircase, the upstairs hall, and the dining room were all covered in sleazy red nylon pile with a design that looked like a lot of fat gold snakes. Then there was the living-room furniture: two chairs, sofa, and hassock upholstered in light-tan imitation leather. In the dining room, a spindly drop-leaf table was opened out and surrounded by six heavy chairs of vaguely ecclesiastical and definitely secondhand appearance. There was also an upright piano. A wrought-iron chandelier hung from the low ceiling, and there were French windows facing a walled square of lawn. The kitchen was presentable, but as we stepped onto the orange plaid linoleum I was filled with homesickness for the bed-sitter in Fitzwilliam Square where I'd lived ten years before. The kitchen there had been a sort of shed built into a corner, though in no way detracting from that beautiful room with its ornate marble fireplace, one tall window, and high carved and gilded ceiling.

"How did you happen to choose this place?" I asked Hope Hazlitt.

She said, "It was exactly midway between Bobby's school and my job in town. Come an upstairs."

On the second floor there were four small bedrooms and a pale-yellow bath. Hope opened the first door on the left and said, "This is Bobby's room." The walls were covered with pictures of English pop singers and American baseball players. She said, "I'm not going to bother doing any cleaning in here. I figured it wouldn't appeal to you." She was absolutely right. We crossed the hall to a much smaller room—suitable, I thought, for the maid. Hope said, "I thought this would suit you."

I said, "What about the others?"

She said, "I use the little room next door as a kind of study." It contained a desk, a file cabinet, and a couple of folding chairs. "Then there's my room." She was ready to pass it by, but I stopped, and so she opened the door. "I won't be cleaning this up, either, so don't bother coming in here. Just leave everything the way it is." This was spoken peremptorily, as much as to say "Keep out." And so after I moved in I made a point, every couple of days, of going in and walking around Hope Hazlitt's bedroom. It was a real boudoir and, true to her word, she hadn't done a thing in the way of tidying up there. Clothes were piled on the red velvet boudoir chair. Shoes stuck out from under the bed, which, beneath a pink satin comforter, was obviously unmade. A hair dryer trailed its cord from the open drawer of an antiqued white night table, and the table itself was covered with curlers. The waste basket was overflowing.

I was amused by all this. Or rather, it amused me to turn the emotional cartwheel it took to go from Hope Hazlitt's vulgar boudoir in that ghastly house in Castle Court out into the sober charm of Booterstown with its grey stone cottages, its vivid gardens. Being a seaside suburb, the place had a holiday air. There was no beach, but people would climb the steps at one end of the seawall to sit on the rocks and sun themselves or go swimming in the shallow water. That was an exceptional July—at least, it would have been exceptional anywhere else. For Ireland it was miraculous. Day after day, the sky was blue, the sun was strong, and there was a wonderful breeze. The pleasure I took in all this, the bliss I felt at being back in Ireland, soon permeated the house in Castle Court. After a couple of days I was quite content there.

When I lived in Dublin before, I made no friends at the College of Art—that is, not among the girls. Love can develop under almost any conditions, but friendship, in its beginnings, requires the right medium, and for me the College of Art was all wrong. I wasn't a full-time student, which set me apart to begin with, and my nationality finished the job. I used to feel that the girls in my classes had an image of me that corresponded to what an old woman I'd met in Mayo must have had in mind when she addressed me as "Yank."

If the boys at the College of Art thought me Yankish,

it didn't seem to matter, and I didn't lack boyfriends in Ireland. Dublin social life was democratic and it flourished after hours. When the pubs closed, word would go out that someone's flat was available, and at the subsequent "party" you'd come across anyone from members of the Dáil to fiddlers up from the country for the day. But the nicest Irishman I met came my way by a roundabout route. One day toward the end of my second year, a letter arrived from someone named Stephen Cronin, who said he was just back from New York, where a girl we both knew had told him to look me up. I didn't particularly like the girl and so I ignored the letter. Two weeks later my doorbell rang; when I answered it, a tall, very thin young man with curly grey hair introduced himself and said, "You didn't answer my note, so I thought I'd come round."

Stephen worked in the publicity office of Aer Lingus. He was appalled at how little I knew of Irish life, apart from the pubs and parties and the College of Art, and he set out to correct the situation; in his little white sports car, we went flying in every direction along the empty Irish roads. He was an ideal guide—well informed, funny, tireless, and above all cultured. He had a passion for Georgian furniture and silver, old Waterford glass, English pictures, Indian carpets, all of which he collected and stored in the basement of his parents' house in Dalkey. I began to envision life among these things, and the vision appealed to me. I'd been in love a lot and always found it harrowing; I was ready for something more civilized. Then one evening Stephen came by in a terrible state. "Forgive me, Ann," he said, "but I must talk to someone."

It's doubly flattering to be chosen as a confidante; you

feel both important and on the verge of becoming more so. I said, "Come on in. I'll make some tea."

Laughing with embarrassment, groaning with real misery, he sat down and launched into a story that floored me. "I've been in love with someone for three years—a Spanish girl who worked in the embassy here. I was never so involved with anyone, but she was very neurotic and used to throw terrible scenes."

I wasn't in love with Stephen but I hadn't ruled out this possibility, and as I listened to him what was uppermost in my mind was covering myself. "What sort of scenes would she make?" I asked.

"She'd quite literally beat her head against the wall."

"What would you do then?"

"Simply walk out."

"What would set her off in the first place?"

"It was mostly that she wanted to live with me and try it out, but I wanted to get married. Otherwise I knew I'd be left high and dry."

"What finally happened?"

"She transferred to London. Now she's come back and says she wants to marry me."

I said, "Do you still want to marry her?"

He didn't. The Spanish girl went home to Barcelona, and Stephen and I continued to go out, but things weren't the same. The illusion was gone, and we spent most of our time together analyzing his previous love affairs: the Norwegian, the Belgian, the Venezuelan, the Israeli—they were all more or less the same type, a little disturbed and very determined. When I came back to New York, we exchanged a few letters, and occasionally he flew over on Aer

Lingus business; I'd wonder then whether something mightn't yet develop between us but I felt that in the light of the Spanish girl I struck him as a bit tame—that was how I struck myself, compared to her—and so I held back. When one Christmas he wrote that he was getting married (surprisingly—for him—to a girl with an Irish surname), I was relieved, though I got the impression that he felt guilty with respect to me. He seemed bent on establishing the image of us as having a unique kind of friendship and after the marriage he kept me posted on his affairs. They bought a house in Monkstown. He wrote, "I hope you'll come over and stay with us. There's plenty of room." Soon there was a baby. "You wouldn't believe what a frightful business it is," he wrote. And then, "Stephen George has a sister, Bianca." In the end I did feel some sort of connection with this unknown family; when I agreed to take Hope Hazlitt's house I wrote and told Stephen, and after I was installed in Castle Court he was the first person I called.

"Ann," he said, "I was delighted to get your letter. When will you come to supper?"

I said, "When would you like?"

There was a high-pitched scream at his end. "No, no, Bianca," he said off to one side, and then to me, "Hang on, will you? Let me talk to Suzanne."

With the toe of my shoe I traced one of the gold snakes on the Castle Court carpet, imagining the sort of carpet where Stephen would be standing and the sort of room— a perfect sort of room.

He came back on the line and said, "How would Wednesday suit you?"

I said, "Wednesday's fine."

"I'll pick you up. Will we say half six?"

"Fine," I said. "Wait'll you see this house."

When he did, he frowned and smiled and shook his head, like someone bearing up well under bad news. I said, "Isn't it awful?"

"It's pretty bad," he said. "All the same, I expect you're comfortable."

I said, "In a horrible sort of way I am."

He looked at his watch. "Can I tear you away?" He no longer had a sports car—he drove a small station wagon now. The weight of family life had fallen on him, and he bore it with a touching mixture of gravity and lightheartedness. "Suzanne is looking forward to meeting you," he said as he turned carefully into the traffic on Rock Road.

I said, "I'm looking forward to meeting her." It would have been truer to say I was curious. I wondered how he'd made out—whether his story had a happy ending or one that was merely acceptable. "I was surprised that you married an Irish girl."

"Suzanne's not typical," he said. "She has a mind of her own."

In my experience, Irish girls always had minds of their own—quick, canny, sometimes generous, usually critical minds. I'd never been particularly comfortable with those girls and I felt in no great hurry to meet another, but Monkstown was practically on top of Booterstown, and it took about three minutes to get to Stephen's house. As we drove up, the front door opened, and two women and four children came out onto the doorstep. One woman was rather matronly. The other was a short, thin girl with the blue eyes, rosy cheeks, and curly black hair that are traditionally called Irish beauty. She proved to be Stephen's wife, which meant that the little girl who looked just like her was Stephen's daughter; the little boy with the long blond bob turned out to be Stephen's son. The two other children were strikingly overweight, and when they and the matronly woman had gone and we'd stepped inside, I for some reason—as a rule I'm not outspoken—brought this up. "I'm glad Stephen George and Bianca are who they are," I said. "Those other children were awfully—"

"Fat!" said Suzanne. "That's all I can think of when they're around. I never get used to it."

"It's my one prejudice, fatness," said Stephen. "I loathe it."

The ice was broken. We were of one mind and off to a good start. Suzanne said, "I've got a couple of things still to do for our supper, Ann. Would you like to help Stephen get the kids ready for bed?"

Stephen George was four and a half, Bianca just three. They were beautiful and full of energy and they took complete advantage of their father as he struggled to get them undressed. "You see what it's like," he said to me, helpless with love and exasperation.

Finally Suzanne came upstairs. "Are you being very bold?" she asked the children. This set off a fresh struggle, but it was the last. Stephen George and Bianca were exhausted. The covers were drawn up over their beds, the light was put out, and we left the room. Suzanne said, "Come see the house, Ann."

I have an impression of that house now rather than a clear image of any part of it. I remember rooms painted wonderful colours—rose red, deep Wedgewood, bright yellow. I see marvellous chests and chairs, the fruits of Stephen's long, profitable bachelorhood—his carpets, his interesting objects, his pictures. One thing stands out in my mind, a series of paintings of some big, serious, creamy-looking sheep shown close up in a dark meadow. They're as clear to me now as if I'd lifted my eyes to them again and again, but in fact I got only a glimpse of those creamy sheep, for they hung in the dining room, and we didn't eat there. A small table had been set up in the drawing room, and this was where we spent the evening, though I can't describe the drawing room, either—probably because I was distracted. We had a good time; we three hit it off. In the middle of dinner, Suzanne put down her fork and said, "I can't believe how different you are from what I expected."

I said, "What did you expect?"

"Someone sort of pale and serious." Stephen blushed and protested. She said to him, "I suppose you were trying to make me jealous—jealous and not jealous. Tearing poor Ann down but letting me know she was in the picture."

I said, "Shame on you, Stephen," but I didn't really mind. That I'd made a contribution to this happy household seemed to entitle me to share the happiness, which is something I don't often feel. I'm not someone who's comfortable as a third, or a fifth, or a fifteenth. I believe people are meant to pair off and I accept the corollary to this: that people who don't pair off, for whatever reason—bad judgment, or bad luck, or some quirkiness of mind or heart—must suffer the consequences. But there was nothing to suffer that night at the Cronins'.

Suzanne said, "Anyway, I'm glad you're not pale and serious."

"But I am," I said. "Serious, anyway."

Stephen said, "The trouble with most people is they're not serious enough."

"Or personal enough, I think," said Suzanne.

I said, "It's a question of technique, isn't it? Knowing when to be one thing or the other and how much."

"One's constantly readjusting," said Suzanne. "God, I hate it! Have some more lasagna, Ann." I passed my plate; she gave me a second helping and said, "Why haven't you got married?"

Stephen laughed in embarrassment, but I wasn't embarrassed. I said, "That's a good question."

"A good question that I suppose doesn't have an answer," said Suzanne.

She needn't have let me off the hook; I had an answer. "Somebody once said to me that when a man isn't married you can't help wondering why, but with a woman it just means she didn't like the people who asked her, and the people she'd have liked didn't ask."

Stephen said, "Do you think that's true today?"

I said, "I think it'll always be true, more or less."

"I wonder," said Suzanne. "We have a friend who's a doctor and has two children, and she positively refuses to marry their father. She says she has quite enough to handle."

"Well," I said, "it's true of me."

"Still and all," said Suzanne, "you should be married."

Stephen said, "You really should, Ann."

"I know. It's odd," I said, "not being. Sometimes it feels a bit like never having been a child."

Suzanne nodded vigorously. "There's that whole area missing."

I said, "I seem to attract the wrong sort of men."

"What sort?" she asked.

"Oh," I said, "people who for some reason think I'm going to give them a bad time. And then I don't."

She shook her head from side to side, slowly, several times. "I know, I know," she said. "I was the same. By the time I met Stephen I was so fed up that I said I'd only just try the marriage and only for three months."

"So you see how lucky I am," said Stephen.

I saw this and something else: to the extent that his happiness was hard-won it was still threatened. Happiness is at best a day-to-day affair, but this was a lucky day, and the luck had something to do with my not being pale and serious. I felt like a piece of missing evidence—the proof that Stephen had had a real choice, which, in turn, enhanced the choice he'd made. I think this was why the three of us got on so well—we had a common interest.

"Look," Suzanne said, "are you doing anything this Saturday?"

I said, "I'm not sure."

"A friend of ours, a cellist, is giving a recital. If you're free, why don't you come along?"

"To be perfectly honest," I said, "things like that—quartets and things—put me to sleep." I wasn't being honest at all. I was hedging, reluctant to wear out my welcome, but the welcome was real and not to be backed away from.

Suzanne said, "What about Sunday? We could do something in the afternoon. Were you ever to the Botanic Gardens?"

Stephen said, "I think I took you there, Ann—just before you left."

I said, "That was the zoo."

"The zoo! What was I thinking of?" He'd been thinking of the Spanish girl. He was probably thinking of her again. I know I was—of her and of the evenings in my flat spent talking out his past and talking away the then present. I really didn't regret any of this but I recognized that possibly the time could have been better spent.

"Anyway, it was a very nice zoo," I said.

"And it's a very nice Botanic Gardens," said Suzanne. "Come for Sunday lunch; then we'll all go off. It's a while since we took the kids to the Gardens."

The kitchen in the Cronins' house was small and it had an old-fashioned look. Doing the dishes there was as pleasant as dinner in the drawing room had been, and when the dishes were finished there was pleasantness left over. "Shall we go for a walk?" Stephen suggested.

Suzanne said, "We could take the dogs over to the strand and give them a run."

I said, "What dogs?"

"Dora and Margo," she said. "They live in the garden."

I said, "Is it all right to leave the children?"

"Oh sure," she said. "We'll only be a minute."

Stephen let himself out the kitchen door and met us in front with a sheepdog and an Airedale. Monkstown strand was only a couple of blocks away, but we drove there with the dogs panting and whining and trying to pace in the back of the station wagon. When they were let loose they began racing up and down the promenade, but Dora, the sheepdog, soon got tired and settled down to a melancholy trot alongside us. Stephen patted her and said, "Poor Dora—she's too old to keep up with Margo, and it drives her mad."

I was struck by that remark. It seemed to me to contain a world of sympathy and understanding—that is to say, sympathy and understanding beyond the requirements of family life—which was the great thing about the Cronins. They weren't as closed off in their intimacy as married couples usually seem to me to be.

On Friday I went down to the country to visit friends who have a farm in Monaghan. I've always lived in the city—I'm happy and at home there—but at that farm I'm happier and more at home than I've ever been anyplace else. You can practically taste the air there; you can hear the stillness. I was supposed to stay one night but I stayed two. Sunday morning I took the bus back to Dublin, stopped in at Castle Court to change my clothes, heard Mass at the big, homely Booterstown church, and then went straight to the Cronins'. This quick succession of drastically different perspectives left me keyed up—in contrast to Stephen, who looked a bit played out when he answered the door. "The children have been outrageous," he said. "It took us half an hour, but we finally got them down for their naps."

I said, "I thought things seemed awfully calm." Things, in fact, seemed not so much calm as cool. Inside, in the hall, I felt as if I were receiving the house's equivalent of a blank look but I told myself it was my imagination. When we walked into the kitchen, I changed my mind again and decided I'd been right the first time.

Suzanne said, "Forgive us if we're a bit droopy, Ann. We

were at the most dreadful party last night. It went on and on and got more and more boring. Both of us drank too much and slept badly."

States of grace or of mere congeniality don't often survive a change of scene or additions to the cast of characters. The events of a couple of days had been bound to bury our pleasant evening, and I blamed myself for not bearing this in mind. "Then today you had to have me," I said.

"Not at all," said Stephen. "We were looking forward to it."

Suzanne said, "Yes. You can put it all out of our minds."

The third person is often called on to provide distraction, to smooth over rough places or otherwise ease family pressures. I set about this task willingly and with a confidence based on long experience and the proven compatibility of the Cronins and myself. "I have a foolproof routine for parties, I said. You stay in one place and talk to anyone who happens to come up to you, no matter who. You'd be surprised at all the people you meet that way."

Suzanne said, "That'd be the trouble."

"It beats dodging around, picking and choosing," I said.

"I suppose you don't feel so morally empty afterward," said Stephen. He had a nice way of sharpening your point without turning it against you.

I said, "Exactly."

Suzanne said, "Stephen, will you open the wine?" She went to the refrigerator and took out a salmon salad, moulded in the shape of a fish and decorated with sliced olives and strips of pimento; it seemed the only thing we could have eaten in that pretty kitchen. "That's your place, Ann." She indicated the middle chair.

I sat down and rested elbows on the inlaid beechwood table. "You can't imagine how good it feels to be in a house like this," I said. "After Castle Court."

"What's exactly's wrong with the place?" asked Susanne.

"For one thing it's too done up." I helped myself to the salad and passed the plate to Stephen.

He smiled and said, "Ann had a great liking for dilapidation."

"I wasn't happy unless the stuffing was coming out of the furniture."

"Well, we all get a bit sentimental that way, don't we?" said Suzanne.

I'd always admired Irish hardheadedness, the national determination to call a heart a bleeding heart even, or maybe especially, when the heart was my own. I said, "I suppose that's what it amounts to."

"The next time you come to Ireland you must stay with us," Stephen said.

At the moment I was glad I hadn't taken him up on that old invitation. It's the hostess who ends up with the guest on her hands, and I'd begun to suspect that Suzanne Cronin and I might have also ended up getting on each other's nerves. I said, "I'm not a very good guest, even with people I'm close to."

Suzanne said, "I don't believe that." She spoke not deprecatingly but in a positive way, as if I'd exaggerated. It occurred to me then that there was something more than tiredness in the air. I wondered if the Cronins had quarrelled, and in the interest of winning myself immunity, even at the cost of my pride, I offered a dreary bit of autobiography. "We lived with my grandmother when I was a child. We couldn't ever have company of our own, and I never really got over it. I'm still self-conscious in other people's houses."

"Families," said Stephen. "My grandfather lived with us when I was a kid. He used to take snuff, and I was so ashamed that I'd tell the other kids it was medicine."

"My grandparents died before I was born," said Suzanne. "I was always jealous of people who had them. Have some bread, Ann." She passed me the board; I cut myself a slice and passed it to Stephen.

"Do you find Dublin much changed?" he asked.

This was a subject I could throw myself into, having thought of little else for days. Watching the bathers at Booterstown, gazing up at my old house in Fitzwilliam Square, mingling with the lunchtime crowd in Stephen's Green, wandering among the shoppers at Brown Thomas, standing on O'Connell Bridge, walking the quays, I'd turned the past and the present over and over in my mind and come to a rather complicated and idiosyncratic conclusion which I was very pleased with and more than happy to air: "Different but not really changed."

"Explain yourself," said Stephen. He loved this kind of talk.

I said, "I get a real sense of how things have kept on going. I mean ordinary things—people having birthdays and getting sick and getting better, or getting mad at each other and making up or holding a grudge; and the whole time everyone running into everyone else on Grafton Street or in the Green. Somehow it all adds up to something that looks practically the same and feels totally different."

"But not changed," said Stephen. He looked puzzled but interested. Suzanne looked bored.

I said, "Maybe it's me. In a lot of ways I've been standing still."

Stephen said, "Some people should. Some people are right the way they are."

I saw then what was wrong. After I'd left the other night, they'd talked about me. Suzanne had said, "Ann's really awfully nice," and Stephen had gone on from there, for that was the trouble with him—he was injudicious. He always had been. He was open and enthusiastic and truthful and he didn't know when to keep quiet. He'd gone on about the Spanish girl with me and he'd undoubtedly gone on about me with his wife. Suzanne would have said, "Why didn't it come off between you two?"

And instead of "We weren't in love," he'd probably answered, "I don't know," or words to that unnecessarily honest and ambiguous effect.

Suzanne got up and put the salad plate on the counter, replacing it with a bowl of fruit. "We stayed up talking about you the other night," she said as she sat down again. "Stephen is awfully fond of you, Ann."

It made me sad and it made me furious. I said, "The truth is, I was always too odd for Stephen's taste."

"But that's what we like about people, isn't it?" she said. "The thing that makes them different is the thing that attracts us."

"I was a little too different." I turned to Stephen for corroboration of what he must have at some point acknowledged to himself.

He said, "I think of you whenever I go down Fitzwilliam."

Into this conversational dead end walked Bianca, crying to herself and rubbing her eyes. Behind her came Stephen George, who looked at the remains of the salad and said, "I want some lunch."

Stephen said, "I think we'll ignore that."

"I want lunch!" said Bianca.

"We're all finished," their mother said. "Besides, you had yours before, you and Stephen George. You had your lovely eggs. Remember?"

Stephen George said, "I don't remember." Bianca began to scream.

I took a pear from the bowl, pushed my chair away from the table, and said to the children, "Take me outside and show me the garden."

Of all the good things about that house, the garden was possibly the best. It was a long stretch of level ground surrounded by a high hedge, with borders of flowers on the two sides and a vegetable garden at the back. There were trees—an apple, a handsome chestnut, a laburnum, and a young elm with a swing attached to one of the branches. Two wooden deckchairs were set up near the house; when my eyes adjusted to the sunlight I noticed croquet wickets sticking up in the grass. The dogs ran up and jumped all over us and then ran off again. Stephen George said to me, "Do you want to see the game?"

I thought he probably wanted to play croquet and I said, "Sure."

He led me to the back of the garden, where a short, sturdy flight of wooden stairs stood against the hedge; we climbed the stairs to what was a small private grandstand looking out on a playing field. A cricket match was in progress. Stephen George and I watched for a minute or two; then he said, "Would you like to swing?"

I translated this as "I'd like to swing," and said, "Sure." But Bianca had got there first. I said, "How about a push, Bianca?" She stood up and sat down again, but the swing was slightly off balance, and my first hesitant push made it zigzag; Bianca began to scream. I steadied the swing, and she jumped off and ran into the house.

"Now it's my turn," Stephen George said with innocent satisfaction.

I'd sent him up half a dozen times when his father came out into the garden and strolled over to us. Stephen looked preoccupied and a little sheepish, and so the change of plan he proposed came as no surprise, though I was irritated by the way he put it: "Do you feel like going to the Botanic Gardens?" It was as if it were a brainstorm he'd just had, and from this I gathered that the plan had already been rejected. I felt a little left out, a little in the way, and no less so for the recognition that the feeling was unreasonable, since I no longer had any desire to go to the Botanic Gardens.

"Why don't we skip it?" I said.

"It's difficult with the children," he explained. "When they start acting up, there's not much you can do."

I said, "Don't be silly. They're fine children."

"We might sit out here and relax," he suggested.

"That's just what I feel like doing." Sunbathing is conducive to silence, and I was tired of making conversation, tired of being taken the wrong way.

Suzanne came out in a bikini. "Would you like to borrow one?" she asked. I declined, feeling overly fastidious, which I probably am. Stephen brought out another deck chair and set it up; then he inflated and filled a plastic wading pool for the children, who took off their clothes and began to dash in and out of the water. "Watch me!" they cried as they bellyflopped or lay on their stomachs splashing each other. The dogs retreated to the far end of the garden and lay down under the trees, though every so often Margo, the Airedale, would get up and make a frantic circuit of the yard, while poor Dora looked on, her rheumy old eyes full of despair. In this desultory but slightly hectic fashion, an hour passed, then another hour. Finally the sun went behind the trees, and I sat forward.

"I'd better be going," I said.

Suzanne said, "Won't you stay for tea?"

The offer was a formality, a way of keeping up the appearance of friendship, when in fact we'd had more than enough of each other's company. For the same reason and also for the sake of my self-respect, I made an offer of my own. "Why don't you come back and have tea with me? You could see the famous house." This plan offered activity, distraction, and a change of scene, which made it seem, at that point, like a good idea, or at least the better one. The children were dressed, Suzanne changed into a skirt and blouse, Stephen put on a sweater, and we climbed into the car and drove to Castle Court. In the strong late-afternoon light the twelve white houses stood out like twelve sore thumbs.

"My God!" said Suzanne.

"The last one on the right," I reminded Stephen. He circled the development and came to a stop at the end house. Suzanne said, "It's all very mock Georgian."

"More like mock Levittown," I said. Stephen, knowing something of America, laughed.

"Well, anyway, it's very mock," said Suzanne.

She began to rub me the wrong way. It wasn't as if I were to blame for the flareup of Stephen's interest in me. It wasn't even as if that interest meant anything—it was a simple reflex, as inconsequential as the blink of an eye. Still, I could see her side of it—balance is crucial to marriage, and if I'd tipped the balance then I had to go. It was cut and dried and had nothing to do with me personally. The recognition of this revived something in me—my sense of proportion, my sense of humor. I said, "Ta-da!" and opened the front door and let them in.

"Suzanne turned in a circle, took everything in, and said, "How hideous!" In her, too, something had suddenly revived—the authority that was hers by virtue of the beautiful house in Monkstown. She led the way into the Castle Court living room, turned another circle, and said, "It's perfectly hideous." The children, running from room to room, found the piano and began to bang on the keyboard; the noise drew us to the dining room. Suzanne looked out the French windows at the neat patch of grass and shook her head in disbelief. "You'd think there'd at least be a few marigolds."

I said, "You would, wouldn't you?"

She shuddered. "I couldn't live in a place like this."

I said, "I think of it as just a place I'm staying."

She said, "I couldn't *stay* in a place like this. I'd be too depressed."

I said, "I can't afford to get depressed. I'm stuck here."

"I'd get out of it somehow," she insisted. "I'd go to a hotel."

"I can't afford that, either." My sense of humor began to give way again. I said, "You don't want to go upstairs, do you?"

"Let's," she said.

And so I led them up to the second floor and showed them my little cell, Bobby's bedroom, the pale-yellow bath, Hope Hazlitt's study. The boudoir door was closed. "What's in there?" asked Suzanne.

I said, "The master bedroom." She opened the door and gave a little gasp.

"More of a mistress's bedroom," said Stephen.

Suzanne said, "It's positively decadent."

"It is, isn't it?" I said.

Stephen stepped over the threshold and surveyed the room, mentally taking its measure. "It's a good size," he concluded and stepped back into the hall.

"Yes, said Suzanne. "Why aren't you using this one?"

I said, "I was told not to." I closed the door on the pink satin comforter, the unmade bed, the boudoir chair, the dirty clothes, the curlers. "What about tea?" I asked them.

Suzanne said, "Thank you, Ann, but I think we'll move along—though I'd love a glass of water."

We went back downstairs to the kitchen, where Stephen George and Bianca had got hold of a bag of mints I'd left on the table. "Please put those back," said their father.

"Can't they have one?" I asked.

Susanne and Stephen exchanged a look that was both discreet and thoroughly intimate—the house had done the trick. They'd begun to remember what they meant to each other and what they'd done for each other—she, thanks to him, and he, thanks to her, would in all probability never be faced with so desolate a prospect as that house in Castle Court. "Maybe just one mint apiece," Stephen said. Stephen George took a mint for himself and one for his sister, unwrapped them, and threw the papers on the floor.

"Pick up the sweet papers," Stephen said. Bianca dropped her mint and began to cry. "May she have another, Ann?" asked Stephen.

I said, "Sure."

Bianca grabbed the bag and threw the mints on the floor. Mortified and amused, Stephen said, "We'd best be going."

I walked them to the door. "How much longer will you be here?" asked Suzanne.

I said, "Another three weeks."

"We must see each other again," she said. "We might have lunch in town one day."

I said, "Yes," but I doubted that we'd be having lunch in town or anything else. It would only be a repetition of the afternoon we'd just spent together—another skirmish in an undeclarable war of which I had to end up the loser, as I was the loser now. But if you're going to be a loser you might as well be a good one, you might as well play the part. I followed them outside and stood on the doorstep with my arms folded across my chest, my head slightly tilted. I made a pathetic picture, standing there alone in front of that awful house, but I wasn't as pathetic as I looked. Nor were the Cronins, as they slammed and locked their car doors, so very safe. For, with all the resources it has to command, happiness remains a shaky fortress. Sorrow is the stronghold.

The Homesick Industry

Hugo Hamilton

I'VE GOT A JOB in the city now, in a company that manufactures Irish products, both for the home market and for the export. Traditional music, language lessons, dancing records, tin whistles, Aran sweaters—the lot. I'm the distribution manager, so I can see these products being sent all over the world. Even as far away as China, there are homesick people who think of Ireland every day. People tearing the paper off to take out the books and start

HUGO HAMILTON (1953–) was born in Dublin of Irish-German parentage. He has brought elements of his mixed language identities to novels such as *Surrogate City* (1990), *The Last Shot* (1991), *The Love Test* (1995), *Headbanger* (1996), and *Sad Bastard* (1998). His short stories have been collected as *Dublin Where the Palm Trees Grow* (1996). A memoir of his Irish-German childhood was published as *The Speckled People* (2003) with a sequel in 2006—*The Sailor in the Wardrobe*. In 1992 Hamilton was awarded the Rooney Prize for Irish Literature. *Sang impur,* the French translation of *The Speckled People,* won the Prix Femina Etranger in 2003 and *Il cane che abbaiava alle onde,* the Italian translation of the memoir, won the Premio Giuseppe Berto in 2004. Hamilton lives in Dublin.

speaking Irish again like babies. People in tropical places like Cairns, Australia, sitting under palm trees in the heat with the sound of strange birds all around them, putting on the dancing CDs and working out the steps—one, two, three, one, two, three. For a moment, you get the impression that the whole world is homesick. I can see them up there in Alaska, wearing thick Aran sweaters under their parkas and holding small tin whistles to their frozen lips. Frozen fingers pressing out the first warped notes and bringing back the faraway feeling of home.

Nothing has changed very much and I sometimes get the impression that I am like my father when he was alive. I might as well be him. I get on the train every morning and sit down with the newspaper. I see the same people around me in the carriage, the same variation of faces, the same silence, the same glances avoiding each other. I get to the office and go into dream, drifting away to remote places.

People would say that's the way the world carries on from one generation to the next, father and son, into infinity. They will think I have just stepped into my father's shoes. Here he comes, they will say, carrying a cool, new shoulder bag instead of his usual briefcase. He's looking younger, they might say, but apart from the shoes and the hair, apart from the general youthful swagger and the fact that I don't wear glasses like he did, nothing has moved on at all. I have the same forehead, the same hands, the same smile. I have the same history and I have become my father in every respect, which is what I had always hoped to avoid.

I have always refused to be like him. I wanted to be different, to travel, to forget where I come from. But sometimes when you try that hard, you just end up being the same without noticing it. You finally surrender to the songs like everyone else. Maybe you sometimes become what you fight against.

I suppose that's why they gave me the job as distribution manager, because they could see that I understood the idea of not belonging. They could see that I had inherited something from my father, in spite of the fact that I had always resisted it.

My boss calls me upstairs to his office one day and demands to know what has gone wrong. He's just like my father in many ways. He has that look of nostalgia in his eyes. His chin quivers when he speaks. He wears a pink shirt and the light on his desk keeps flickering and going out, so he has to tap it with his pen to get it going again. He looks at me under the arch of the light and shows his frustration. He says he hopes I'm not just in the job for the money and I laugh.

"What's that supposed to mean?" he asks.

"What?"

"That laugh?"

"Nothing," I reply.

"You just laughed. I said I hoped you didn't just take on the job for the money and you just laughed. What's so funny?"

"I didn't mean to laugh," I say.

He has something more substantial to talk about. He has ordered a skip which has been delivered outside at the front of the building so that a room at the back of the offices can be cleared. The room is to be used to store a new consignment of knitwear from the West of Ireland. Sweaters that women have been working on for weeks and weeks will shortly be arriving here, destined mostly for the export market. For tourists arriving in the summer, for airport shops and various outlets around the capital. In the meantime, we need to make storage space. He wants to streamline the knitwear operation, so that it's knitter to wearer in the shortest possible time.

But there is a problem, because my boss thinks I'm going to physically go in there with my staff and carry out all those dusty files and printing junk to the skip. He says it's urgent. He describes it as a crisis. A policeman on a motorbike has already called into the reception to ask how long it's going to take. The skip is taking up an entire lane of traffic. But I've refused to do this kind of work. It's not my duty. I will not be ordered to fill a skip. Skips are not my responsibility.

So here I am in his office once again, staring across his desk. He's wearing the same pink shirt as always, or else he must have a hundred pink shirts which he bought in one place because he likes them so much. He fiddles with the desk lamp again because he can't see me. He's blinded himself as if in self-interrogation.

"Are you afraid of work?" he wants to know.

"I'm not a laborer," I reply.

He frowns when he laughs. He laughs when you think he should be getting angry. I want to ask him what's so funny, but he's already leaning across the desk, looking at me in the eye.

"If you could only see yourself," he says.

He smiles. He slaps his desk and looks out the window. Then he looks back and starts shaking his head.

"I wish I had a mirror so you could see yourself," he says.

I am the portrait of refusal.

Suddenly, he looks at the evening paper on his desk. He asks me what star sign I belong to, but I refuse to enter into this new game.

"Your birthday is this month, isn't it?"

I don't answer. I know this comradeship trick.

"Capricorn, right?"

He reads out the generic little piece of fortune-telling from the paper. "You will find that your social life will improve dramatically later on this week."

"Is that all?" I ask.

He smiles and tries to appeal to me as a friend. He's in a bit of a spot, he explains. Could I not make the exception for once? He tells me that he will never ask me to do anything like this again, that it's only because of the extreme urgency of the situation, the traffic outside. It's not the way he would have liked it, but the gardaí have been in a second time, demanding that the skip should be removed.

"I'm not doing it," I say.

"Please," he begs. "Just this once."

"You can find somebody else to do this kind of work."

He stares at me across the table for a while longer. I can see his disappointment. He tries something else. He talks about moral responsibility, duty, dedication, laziness.

"Anarchy?" he suddenly shouts. "Is that what you want?" It descends into a political argument. He talks about a more equitable, a more socialist society, a fairer, Irish-speaking country. He doesn't let up. He wants a country like the Blasket Islands with nobody owning anything any more than anyone else.

"Nobody owning anything at all," I say.

He leans forward to make his point. There was a ship-wreck on the Great Blasket once, he tells me, and some boys on the island found a casket full of brand new watches. They wanted to keep them for themselves and hid them in a cave. But they were not accustomed to owning anything or having any personal possessions, so by the end of the day, they had given them all away and everyone on the island was wearing a watch, even though they had no real use for them and nobody had any sense of time on the island.

He tries to fix the flickering desk lamp for good this time. He says it's not really socialism he's after at all but democracy. He says democracy is everybody doing their share regardless of what rank or position they hold. It's people paying their fare on buses.

"That's what democracy is," he says. "People respecting their country and working for each other."

Suddenly he loses it. He burns his hand against the shade of the desk lamp. He gets up from his chair in a fury and flicks his wrist around the room. But it's only when he looks out through the window at the empty skip outside and all the cars snaking around it that he remembers why I had come to his office in the first place. Not a single thing thrown into the skip yet, while we're arguing about the solution for Ireland.

"I'll show you," he says. "Follow me."

I follow him down the stairs, all the way down from the third floor, passing by people without saying a word all the way down to the offices at the back of the building. He takes off his tie and puts it into his pocket. He rolls up his pink sleeves and lifts up the rubbish in his hands, old files, printing materials, ink canisters. Out into the street he goes, carrying bits of junk and throwing them into the skip. I stand there and watch him, refusing to touch anything. He doesn't say a word. His hands are black. His pink shirt has gone grey and there are black streaks on his face from some old printing ink. He's sweating and breathing heavily.

I join in and start carrying things out with him. We work in silence, me carrying out the same amount as him, no more and no less, until the skip is full and we both go our separate ways, him back to his office upstairs and me back into the dispatch office in the basement. He doesn't give me those triumphant looks. He doesn't rub it in. If anything, he understands that I am hurt by this, and defeated.

A few minutes later the phone rings. I pick it up and wait. But there's nothing. It's the two of us listening to each other in silence. Then he finally speaks.

"I'll make it up to you," he says.

But I've put it all behind me. By the following day it's forgotten. The Aran sweaters begin to arrive in big boxes. Larger consignments are on the way. We are overwhelmed by orders coming in and can hardly even keep up with the demand. Knitwear going out to addresses everywhere around the globe, Canada and the USA, France and Denmark, even Italy.

And one day not long after that, it's my birthday. My boss wants to show that he hasn't forgotten. He's a man who keeps his word and comes down in the afternoon with a gift. He and his secretary and two or three others from the department crowd around me in my office with a big parcel wrapped in blue paper. They clap and wish me a happy birthday in Irish.

'*Lá breithe shona dhuit,*' they say, all smiling, as they hand me the gift. They wait for me to open it, but I'm so surprised by all this kindness that I can only stare at the blue paper.

"Thanks," I say.

"Aren't you going to open it?" my boss says.

I begin to take off the paper. I can smell what's inside before I can even see it. The familiar smell of rough wool is unmistakable. It's one of the hand-knit, Inishfree Aran sweaters that I've been sending out to so many people abroad. And now, one of them seems to have come back to me as a birthday gift. A big brown, rope-patterned Aran sweater with a ringed collar.

"You shouldn't have," I stammer

For a moment, I ask myself if this is some kind of big joke they're playing on me, but they are all very serious.

"Are you going to put it on?" my boss says.

So I thank them again and again, and put it on out of politeness. I can smell the oily sheep's wool all over me and I suddenly feel suffocated. I used to wear one of these big sweaters as a boy. My father bought them for us. My father wore one himself. It's making me ill and I'm already thinking of what to do with it, how to get out of the building without them noticing that I've left it behind. When they finally leave, I wait for a moment before taking it off and replacing it in the plastic wrapper. I put it back with all the other jumpers waiting to go out in all directions, all over the world. Some days later it goes out by post to Spain, to an address in Madrid.

A Visit to Newgrange

Éilís Ní Dhuibhne

MUTTI WROTE TO ERICH. She would like to visit him
in May. It had been two years since his last holiday in Bad
Schwarzstadt and she was missing him. Besides, she was
longing to see Ireland. A poster in the village travel agency
depicted a scene in Connemara: a lake and hills and a don-
key. The hills were so very green, she could hardly wait to
climb them. And the sky was so very blue. And the don-
key, so very friendly. It confirmed for her what she had

ÉILÍS NÍ DHUIBHNE (1954–) was born in Dublin. Her
works include short story collections such as *Blood and Water*
(1982) and *The Inland Ice and Other Stories* (1997). Other works
worth noting are *The Bray House* (1990), *The Uncommon Cor-
morant* (1990), and *Eating Women Is Not Recommended* (1991).
The Pale Gold of Alaska and Other Stories was published in 2000
and *Midwife to the Fairies: Selected Stories* was published in 2002.
She received Arts Council Bursaries in Literature in 1986 and
1998. Other awards and prizes include the Readers Association
of Ireland Award, the Bisto Book of the Year Award, the Stew-
art Parker Award, and an Oireachtas award. Ní Dhuibhne works
in the National Library of Ireland and lives in County Dublin
with her husband and two children.

always known, in her heart, about Ireland. She would arrive at 1:23 P.M. on the fourteenth, flight E4327. Perhaps Erich could spare a few hours from his studies to come and meet her? She realized that he was very busy and if he couldn't manage it, why, she wouldn't mind. She was used to travelling alone now, ever since Vatti died (fifteen years previously). It was true that she was sixty-eight and suffered from severe arthritis of the hip. But she could get along very well on her own. Her English, at least, was rather good. That much she had to admit. She'd been taking lessons all winter, at the Bad Schwarzstadt Adult Education Center. Of course, she'd never been to an English-speaking country before. Not since before the War, anyway, when she had stayed with a family in Devon, improving her command of the language. The father had been a doctor. He had died on D-Day, tending the wounded on a French beach.

She had written a long letter, apparently. I didn't see it myself. Erich relayed its contents to me, in a light, satirical tone he sometimes uses for comic effect. Probably he embroidered the details as he went along: he has a wonderful imagination.

Underneath his soft chuckles, however, lay a core of hysteria so blatant that I knew I was meant to take heed of it. Fear, I supposed it must be. Of Mutti. She was a little domineering, he had mentioned, once or twice? Oh, yes, indeed. With knobs on (Erich, like many speakers of English as a foreign language, possesses a rich store of colloquial expressions, and cannot resist employing them whenever possible). She was a real old battle-axe. Hard as nails. More demanding than a two-year-old ayatollah. More conservative than Maggie Thatcher. A dyed-in-the-wool Lutheran. More puritanical than John Knox.

I would have to move out.

It was only temporary.

She didn't realize he was living with me and the shock would be too much for her. Her only son. It was only for two weeks. Why make an issue of it? For a mere fortnight.

What about my mother? I politely enquired. She was dyed-in-the-wool Catholic, more conservative than John Paul II, more puritanical than the archbishop of Dublin. She'd had to turn a blind eye on the fact that her daughter, her favourite daughter, her fifth daughter, was living in a state of mortal sin. She'd had to accept that life was different in Germany, different in Ranelagh, and soon would be different in Tuam, County Galway. And what about me, for heaven's sake? I was a dyed-in-the-wool Catholic, too, when you came to think about it. Not just dyed, blued. Blued in the delicate, gauzy wool of the Virgin Mary's cloak: her blue-white, whiter-than-ordinary-white, artistically-draped, archetypal emblem of purity. A Child of Mary, that's what I actually was, called to her service in the chapel of Loreto on the Green when already a nubile impressionable fifteen-year-old. What about that? And what about integrity, courage, and honesty, qualities which Erich claimed to prize above all others?

Mutti was sixty-eight. She had severe arthritis of the hip. It was only for two weeks. For heaven's sake.

On the thirteenth of May, I moved in with Jacinta who lives around the corner. On the fifteenth, Erich invited me up for a cup of tea, and I was introduced to Mutti.

She moved swiftly towards me, hobbling a little on the

hip, and encircled me in a warm embrace. I don't hug people's mothers, or touch them at all if I can avoid it, and I was put off guard. Oblivious of my confusion, she smiled radiantly, and effused:

"It is so nice to see you! Erich tells me all about you this morning. Such a nice surprise for me! I did not know Erich has a girlfriend, you see. In Ireland, that is!"

I shook her hand gently: slight, bony and hot, two rocky protrusions on its third tinger bit into my palm. I held on for a second, and examined Mutti. She was about five feet tall and fragile, with bountiful curly grey hair, large gentian eyes, innumerable glittering teeth. A bygone beauty. "Bygone" in my estimation, that is, although probably not in her own, if my experience of her type is anything to go on.

"Now, we have a nice cup of tea!"

She had motioned me towards the sofa, a handsome tweed one which I had bought the winter before in Kilkenny Design. We sat down, and Erich put on the kettle. Just a cup of tea. They'd had dinner in town, he explained. Yes, yes, acquiesced Mutti, such an excellent meal. I had not had dinner in town. I'd had nothing since lunch, and then I'd had two crispbreads and a slice of cheese.

I glared at Erich behind her back and he lilted: "Perhaps you'd like a sandwich? Are you hungry?" "Oh not at all," I replied icily. "Don't go to any trouble on my account." My bitterness was wasted on him: he has weather-proof sensibilities, and can, at the flick of some interior zip, protect himself from all atmospheric variation. (This ability is one of the qualities which encouraged me to love him.) Blithely, he placed three mugs of tea, weak and tasteless, on the coffee table. We sipped it slowly, he and I marshalled up on the sofa opposite Mutti, who began her maneuvers in oral English by requesting that I call her Friederika (I'd die first). Then she gave a full report of her trip from Germany and of the sightseeing tour she had taken that day. Questions of greater significance followed: Were my parents still alive? What did my father do for a living? What was my own occupation? Rank? Salary? Quick but efficient. The cross-examination over, we ceded to her command that we watch television, since this would aid her in her battle with the language. Before I left, it was arranged that I should collect both Mutti and Erich the following morning and drive them to Newgrange, which Erich considered an essential ingredient of any Irish tour worth its salt, as he put it himself. Mutti had clapped her hands at the suggestion.

"Oh, yes. That would be so nice! Newgrange. I think Herr Müller mentions it. Is it near Spiddal?"

A month prior to her visit, Mutti had borrowed a guidebook from the public library in Bad Schwarzstadt. The work of one Heinrich Müller, it was entitled *Ein kleines irisches Reisebuch*, and she had studied it with single-minded diligence until she knew its contents by heart. It was to be her inseparable vade mecum during her holiday, and her main criterion for enjoyment in sightseeing was that the sight had been referred to by Herr Müller.

Therefore she had merrily and gratefully limped through the litter of O'Connell Street ("Oh! the widest street in Ireland!"), but the Powerscourt Centre had failed to arouse the mildest commendation. The Book of Kells had won her freshest laurels, but to the "Treasures of Ireland" exhibition, her reaction was one of chilled disappointment. "Please,

what is the meaning of the word 'treasure'?" she had asked
Erich, coming out of the museum onto Kildare Street. "We
did not have it in class, I believe."

Herr Müller had spent the greater part of his *Reise* in
Spiddal, and had devoted more than half his book, ten
whole pages, to a graphic account of that settlement and
its environs. Few corners of the western village were unfamiliar to Mutti, and she anticipated her sojourn there
loudly and often and with the greatest of pleasure. Unfor-
tunately, it would occur at the end of her stay in Dublin
and last for no more than two days.

I arrived at the flat on the following morning, having taken
a day's leave from my job in the Department of Finance.

"We'll go through the Phoenix Park," I recommended
brightly, determined to get value for my time. "It's much
more interesting that way, and only a bit longer. The pres-
ident lives there. It's the biggest park in Europe."

"Ah, yes," responded Mutti noncommittally, as she settled into the passenger seat and opened a map. "Can you
show me where it is?"

I tried to lean across the brake and locate it for her, but
Erich beat me to it, and, from the rear, indicated the rele-
vant green patch. Mutti took a pencil from her handbag,
held it poised in midair, and smiled: "Are we going now?"
On, James.

I drove to Charlemont Bridge.

"That's the canal," I exclaimed brilliantly, waving at it as
we turned off Ranelagh Road.

"Canal?"

"You know, Mutti. Canal. Not a river. Made by man. *Ein Kanal.*" Erich preferred the translation with caution: Mutti had decreed that no German be spoken in her presence, since this might sabotage her chances of commanding the language.

"It's called the Grand Canal," I continued, pedantically. "There are two canals in Dublin, the Royal and the Grand. This is the Grand. It's quite a famous canal, actually. Poems have been written about it. Good poems. Quite well-known poems."

Alas, it was not the leafy-with-love part of canal, it was the grotesque-with-graffiti bit, and Mutti stared, bemused, at peeling mildewed walls and disintegrating furry corpses. Even if it had been picturesque, I don't think its high-falutin' associations would have pulled any weight: Kavanagh had the misfortune to be post-Müller.

We drove towards Kilmainham in silence. The looming jail flooded my spirits with enthusiasm. The Struggle for Freedom was a favourite theme of Heinrich's, and Mutti, I had gathered from a few comments she had made, had also fallen victim to the romantic nostalgia for things Irish, historical, and bloody.

"Look!" I cried, "there's Kilmain. . . ." But she had glimpsed the portico of the boys' school, which is impressive. And fake.

"Oh, Erich! How nice! Is it medieval, do you think?"

"Oh, yes, I think so, Mutti," replied Erich, in his most learned voice. He knows nothing about Dublin, or architecture, or the Middle Ages.

"It looks like some of our German castles."

"Look," I pressed, "that's Kilmainham Jail. The 1916 leaders were imprisoned there." The light turned green. "And shot," I added, optimistically.

"In Bad Schwarzstadt we have two castles dating from the thirteenth century, Eileen, Marienschloss and Karlsschloss. They are so nice. People come to look from everywhere."

"Really? I'd love to see them some day!"

The hint was ignored. I turned into the park by the Islandbridge gate.

"This is the Phoenix Park," the guided tour continued.

"Oh! A park. And we may drive in it. How nice." Her tone was deeply disapproving. "In Germany, we have many car-free zones. You know. Green zones, they are called. It is good without cars sometimes. For the health."

At that moment, a Volkswagen sped around one of the vicious bends which are so common on the charming backroads of the park. It took me unawares, and I was forced to swerve in order to avoid it. Swerve very slightly, and the Volkswagen was at fault.

"Oh, oh, oh, oh!" screamed Mutti, dapping her hands across her face. Through bony fingers her gentian eyes glared vindictively at me. I gritted my teeth and counted to fifty. Then I repeated fifty times "a man's mouth often broke his nose," a proverb I had come across in *The Connaught Leader* a few weeks previously. Meanwhile, Mutti ignored the Pope's Cross, the lovely woods, the flocks of deer gambolling in the lovely woods, the American Embassy, the troops of travellers' ponies bouncing off the bonnet, the polo grounds and Áras an Uachtaráin.

"What town will we come to next?"

"Castleknock," between one "a man's mouth" and the next.

Scratch, scratch, went the pen on the map. Scratch scratch, through Blanchardstown, Mulhuddart, Dun-shaughlin, Trim, past a countryside resplendent with frilly hedgerows, full-cream buttercups, fairy queen hawthorn, and, flouncing about everywhere, iridescent, giggling, fresh-from-Paris foliage. The sort of surrounding which sent many a medieval Irish monk into reams of ecstatic alliteration, as I liked to point out to my friends at this time of year, delicately reminding them that, even though I was a faceless civil servant, I had, in my day, sipped at the fountain of the best and most Celtic bards (taking a BA in Old Irish). Today I could practically smell the watercress and hazel. I could have taped the blackbird's song on my cassette. But I did not bother to emphasize the true Gaelic nature of the scenery for Mutti; tactfully leaving her to her own pedantic pursuits. Scritch scratch.

In County Meath we stopped for lunch. "Ah," gasped Mutti appreciatively, outside the "olde worlde" hotel, "this looks nice!" She guessed that an establishment with such a picturesque facade would have a high standard of cuisine. Alas, when we passed the promising threshold our eyes were greeted by a sign stating: "lunch served in the bar," and our nostrils assailed by the ripe seedy odors of grease and alcohol. In Mutti's refined Lutheran opinion, drink was unspeakably Non-U, and her perfect nose wrinkled in disgust.

"Would you like something to drink, Mutti," Erich asked, ordering two pints of Harp with great alacrity.

"Harp? What is that? Lemonade? Juice?"

"Well, no, it's a kind of light beer."

"Juice. I will have some Harp juice, please. I am very thirsty."

When the three drinks arrived, gleaming yellow and foaming over the edges, Mutti first clamped her lips together, then began to sip energetically. Service of the meal was slow, and she tapped her foot impatiently on the carpet.

"It is lucky I am not hungry. They are killing that pig for me, I think."

In twenty minutes, the waitress arrived, bearing a dinner plate for Mutti, covered with slivers of pork and side dishes of carrots and cauliflower and cabbage and potatoes and gravy. She accepted generous helpings of everything . . . "I am not hungry but I pay" . . . and, having dispensed with most of it, slid the leavings into a plastic bag which appeared, as if by magic, from her coat pocket:

"After all, we pay," she said, not bothering to whisper. "I eat this for lunch tomorrow. A little meat, that is all I need, now that I am older. I have a small appetite."

Erich and I finished our salads hastily, and we proceeded to Newgrange.

It does not disappoint. Me. There are many among my acquaintance who hate it. They prefer Knowth and Dowth. Goethe. Shabby Victoriana. Woodworm. I relish the lambent, urbane face of immortality: Newgrange, pretentious crystal palace, lording it over the fat cowlands, the meandering fishbeds, reflecting the glory of the sun without a shadow of suburban modesty.

Erich, although he pays lip service to its archaeological

significance, belongs to the group of those who feel uneasy with this example of prehistoric P.R.; he senses that it is in dubious taste. I would not have been surprised to find Mutti of like mind. But no:

"It is very nice," she gasped, to Erich, as we climbed the hill to the tumulus.

"I knew you'd like it, Mutti," he simpered, his eyes rivetted to the figure of the guide, a slender and provocative one, neatly glazed in luminous yellow pants and white T-shirt. She posed on a standing stone outside the mound and outlined its history in a few well-chosen words, then led the creeping party of tourists along the narrow passage to the burial chamber. Mutti had been pleased by the outside of the grave, but she was in raptures within. The ice-cold room at the center of the hill enchanted her soul, and she oohed and aahed so convincingly that the lemon-clad one directed her remarks expressly at her, catching her large eyes and ignoring the other, less charming, members of the little group. When her spiel was over and she made the mandatory request for questions, only one was asked, and that by Mutti:

"Are there any runic stones here?" How silly, I thought. But, of course, there were. It was possible that one stone at the side of the vault contained writing. Had the guide invented this titbit to satisfy Mutti? Hardly. She had an honest, if tarty, face.

After the tour, Mutti and I lingered in the burial chamber. The others left, gradually, but she seemed to want to stay, and I felt it my duty to remain, too. What with her arthritis. Gradually, however, I realized that I was happy to be in the cool greyness of the place. It has, I noticed for the first time, a curious intimacy, the character of a kitchen, a space at the center of the home where people gather to sustain themselves. To survive. And, although it is as chill as a tomb . . . it is a tomb, after all . . . this room has a hearth, a focus: the guide had explained that once a year the sun would pour through the opening in the outer wall, stream along the entrance passage, and flood the chamber with light. Illumination for the immortal dead.

Mutti, tracing with her delicate fingers the spiralling patterns on the tombstones, turned to me:

"Imagine how nice it is here on December twenty-one. So very nice!"

Her eyes glowed with a candor they had not held before, and for the first time since our meeting we looked at each other full in the face. We laughed. Mutti moved towards me slowly, because of the hip, and I had an impulse to run and embrace her, to kiss her. She would not have been embarrassed, that was the sort of thing she did. But I do not kiss people's mothers, or touch anyone at all, if I can avoid it. So I hesitated.

Erich crept into the chamber. Mutti hobbled over to him and clasped his hand.

"It's time to go," he said. "Haven't you had enough of this creepy old mausoleum?"

So brief are our moments of salvation. So sudden. So easily lost.

The American Wife

Frank O'Connor

ELSIE COLLEARY, who was on a visit to her cousins in Cork, was a mystery even to them. Her father, Jack Colleary's brother, had emigrated when he was a kid and done well for himself; he had made his money in the liquor business, and left it to go into wholesale produce when Elsie was growing up, because he didn't think it was the right background for a girl. He had given her the best of educations, and all he had got out of it was to have Elsie telling

FRANK O'CONNOR (1903–1966) was born in Cork City and produced over 150 works. O'Connor is best known for his short stories in such collections as *Guests of the Nation* (1931), *The Stories of Frank O'Connor* (1952), *My Oedipus Complex and Other Stories* (1963), *Collection Two* (1964), *Collection Three* (1969), *A Set of Variations* (1969), and *Collected Stories* Volume I and II in 1990/ 1991. Some topographical works include *Irish Miles* (1947) and *A Picture Book* (1943). For an account of his early years see *An Only Child* (1961). He also produced numerous translations from the Irish including his translation of *Cúirt an Mheán Oíche*. O'Connor had a stroke while teaching at Stanford University in 1961. He later died from a heart attack in Dublin on March 10, 1966.

him that Irishmen were more manly, and that even Irish-Americans let their wives boss them too much. What she meant was that *he* let her mother boss him, and she had learned from other Irish people that this was not the custom at home. Maybe Mike Colleary, like a lot of other Americans, did give the impression of yielding too much to his wife, but that was because she thought she knew more about things than he did, and he was too softhearted to disillusion her. No doubt the Americans, experienced in nostalgia, took Elsie's glorification of Irishmen good-humoredly, but it did not go down too well in Cork, where the men stood in perpetual contemplation of the dangers of marriage, like cranes standing on one leg at the edge of the windy water.

She stood out at the Collearys' quiet little parties, with her high waist and wide skirts, taking the men out to sit on the stairs while she argued with them about religion and politics. Women having occasion to go upstairs thought this very forward, but some of the men found it a pleasant relief. Besides, like all Americans, she was probably a millionaire, and the most unworldly of men can get a kick out of flirting with a real millionaire.

The man she finally fell in love with did not sit on the stairs with her at all, though, like her, he was interested in religion and politics. This was a chap called Tom Barry. Tom was thirty-five, tall and thin and good-looking, and he lived with his mother and two good-looking sisters in a tiny house near the Barrack, and he couldn't even go for a walk in the evening without the three of them lining up in the hallway to present him with his hat, his gloves, and his clean handkerchief. He had a small job in the courthouse, and was not without ambition; he had engaged in several small business enterprises with his friend Jerry Coakley, but all they had ever got out of these was some good stories. Jerry was forty, and *he* had an old mother who insisted on putting his socks on for him.

Elsie's cousins warned her against setting her cap at Tom, but this only seemed to make her worse. "I guess I'll have to seduce him," she replied airily, and her cousins, who had never known a well-bred Catholic girl to talk like that, were shocked. She shocked them even more before she was done. She called at his house when she knew he wasn't there and deluded his innocent mother and sisters into believing that she didn't have designs on him; she badgered Tom to death at the office, gave him presents, and even hired a car to take him for drives.

They weren't the only ones who were shocked. Tom was shocked himself when she asked him point-blank how much he earned. However, he put that down to unworldliness and told her.

"But that's not even a street-cleaner's wages at home," she said indignantly.

"I'm sure, Elsie," he said sadly. "But then, of course, money isn't everything."

"No, and Ireland isn't everything," she replied. It was peculiar, but from their first evening together she had never ceased talking about America to him—the summer heat, and the crickets chattering, and the leaves alive with fireflies. During her discussions on the stairs, she had apparently discovered a great many things wrong with Ireland, and Tom, with a sort of mournful pleasure, kept adding to them.

"Oh, I know, I know," he said regretfully.

"Then if you know, why don't you do something about it?"

"Ah, well, I suppose it's habit, Elsie," he said, as though he wasn't quite sure. "I suppose I'm too old to learn new tricks."

But Elsie doubted if it was really habit, and it perplexed her that a man so clever and conscientious could at the same time be so lacking in initiative. She explained it finally to herself in terms of an attachment to his mother that was neither natural nor healthy. Elsie was a girl who loved explanations.

On their third outing she had proposed to him, and he was so astonished that he burst out laughing, and continued to laugh whenever he thought of it again. Elsie herself couldn't see anything to laugh at in it. Having been proposed to by men who were younger and better-looking and better off than he was, she felt she had been conferring an honor on him. But he was a curious man, for when she repeated the proposal, he said, with a cold fury that hurt her, "Sometimes I wish you'd think before you talk, Elsie. You know what I earn, and you know it isn't enough to keep a family on. Besides, in case you haven't noticed, I have a mother and two sisters to support."

"You could earn enough to support them in America," she protested.

"And I told you already that I had no intention of going to America."

"I have some money of my own," she said. "It's not much, but it could mean I'd be no burden to you."

"Listen, Elsie," he said, "a man who can't support a wife and children has no business marrying at all. I have no business marrying anyway. I'm not a very cheerful man, and I have a rotten temper."

Elsie went home in tears, and told her astonished uncle that all Irishmen were pansies, and, as he had no notion what pansies were, he shook his head and admitted that it was a terrible country. Then she wrote to Tom and told him that what he needed was not a wife but a psychiatrist. The writing of this gave her great satisfaction, but next morning she realized that her mother would only say she had been silly. Her mother believed that men needed careful handling. The day after, she waited for Tom outside the courthouse, and when he came out she summoned him with two angry blasts on the horn. A rainy sunset was flooding the Western Road with yellow light that made her look old and grim.

"Well," she said bitterly, "I'd hoped I'd never see your miserable face again."

But that extraordinary man only smiled gently and rested his elbows on the window of the car.

"I'm delighted you came," he said. "I was all last night trying to write to you, but I'm not very good at it."

"Oh, so you got my letter?"

"I did, and I'm ashamed to have upset you so much. All I wanted to say was that if you're serious—I mean really serious—about this, I'd be honored."

At first she thought he was mocking her. Then she realized that he wasn't, and she was in such an evil humor that she was tempted to tell him she had changed her mind. Then common sense told her the man would be fool enough to believe her, and after that his pride wouldn't let him propose to her again. It was the price you had to pay for dealing with men who had such a high notion of their own dignity.

"I suppose it depends on whether you love me or not," she replied. "It's a little matter you forgot to mention."

He raised himself from the car window, and in the evening light she saw a look of positive pain on his lean, sad, gentle face. "Ah, I do, but—" he was beginning when she cut him off and told him to get in the car. Whatever he was about to say, she didn't want to hear it.

They settled down in a modern bungalow outside the town, on the edge of the harbor. Elsie's mother, who flew over for the wedding, said dryly that she hoped Elsie would be able to make up to Tom for the loss of his mother's services. In fact, it wasn't long before the Barrys were saying she wasn't, and making remarks about her cooking and her lack of tidiness. But if Tom noticed there was anything wrong, which is improbable, he didn't mention it. Whatever his faults as a sweetheart, he made a good husband. It may have been the affection of a sensitive man for someone he saw as frightened, fluttering, and insecure. It could have been the longing of a frustrated one for someone that seemed to him remote, romantic, and mysterious. But whatever it was, Tom, who had always been God Almighty to his mother and sisters, was extraordinarily patient and understanding with Elsie, and she needed it, because she was often homesick and scared.

Jerry Coakley was a great comfort to her in these fits, for Jerry had a warmth of manner that Tom lacked. He was an insignificant-looking man with a ravaged dyspeptic face and a tubercular complexion, a thin, bitter mouth with bad teeth, and long, lank hair; but he was so sympathetic and

insinuating that at times he even gave you the impression
that he was changing his shape to suit your mood. Elsie
had the feeling that the sense of failure had eaten deeper
into him than into Tom.

At once she started to arrange a match between him and
Tom's elder sister, Annie, in spite of Tom's warnings that
Jerry would never marry till his mother died. When she
realized that Tom was right, she said it was probably as
well, because Annie wouldn't put his socks on him. Later
she admitted that this was unfair, and that it would probably be a great relief to poor Jerry to be allowed to put on
his socks himself. Between Tom and him there was one of
those passionate relationships that spring up in small towns
where society narrows itself down to a handful of erratic
and explosive friendships. There were always people who
weren't talking to other people, and friends had all to be
dragged into the disagreement, no matter how trifling it
might be, and often it happened that the principals had
already become fast friends again when *their* friends were
still ignoring one another in the street. But Jerry and Tom
refused to disagree. Jerry would drop in for a bottle of
stout, and Tom and he would denounce the country, while
Elsie wondered why they could never find anything more
interesting to talk about than stupid priests and crooked
politicians.

Elsie's causes were of a different kind. The charwoman,
Mrs. Dorgan, had six children and a husband who didn't
earn enough to keep them. Elsie concealed from Tom how
much she really paid Mrs. Dorgan, but she couldn't con-
ceal that Mrs. Dorgan wore her clothes, or that she took
the Dorgan family to the seaside in the summer. When

Jerry suggested to Tom that the Dorgans might be doing too well out of Elsie, Tom replied, "Even if they were, Jerry, I wouldn't interfere. If 'tis people's nature to be generous, you must let them be generous."

For Tom's causes she had less patience. "Oh, why don't you people do something about it, instead of talking?" she cried.

"What could you do, Elsie?" asked Jerry.

"At least you could show them up," said Elsie.

"Why, Elsie?" he asked with his mournful smile. "Were you thinking of starting a paper?"

"Then, if you can't do anything about it, shut up!" she said. "You and Tom seem to get some queer masochistic pleasure out of these people."

"Begor, Elsie, you might have something there," Jerry said, nodding ruefully.

"Oh, we adore them," Tom said mockingly.

"You do," she said. "I've seen you. You sit here night after night denouncing them, and then when one of them gets sick you're round to the house to see if there's anything you can do for him, and when he dies you start a collection for his wife and family. You make me sick." Then she stamped out to the kitchen.

Jerry hunched his shoulders and exploded in splutters and giggles. He reached out a big paw for a bottle of stout, with the air of someone snaring a rabbit.

"I declare to God, Tom, she has us taped," he said.

"She has you taped anyway," said Tom.

"How's that?"

"She thinks you need an American wife as well."

"Well, now, she mightn't be too far out in that, either,"

said Jerry with a crooked grin. "I often thought it would take something like that."

"She thinks you have *problems,*" said Tom with a snort. Elsie's favorite word gave him the creeps. "She wouldn't be referring to the mother, by any chance?"

For a whole year Elsie had fits of depression because she thought she wasn't going to have a baby, and she saw several doctors, whose advice she repeated in mixed company, to the great embarrassment of everybody except Jerry. After that, for the best part of another year, she had fits of depression because she was going to have a baby, and she informed everybody about that as well, including the occasion of its conception and the probable date of its arrival, and again they were all embarrassed only Jerry. Having reached the age of eighteen before learning that there was any real difference between the sexes, Jerry found all her talk fascinating, and also he realized that Elsie saw nothing immodest in it. It was just that she had an experimental interest in her body and mind. When she gave him bourbon he studied its taste, but when he gave her Irish he studied its effect—it was as simple as that. Jerry, too, liked explanations, but he liked them for their own sake, and not with the intention of doing anything with them. At the same time, Elsie was scared by what she thought was a lack of curiosity on the part of the Cork doctors, and when her mother learned this she began to press Elsie to have the baby in America, where she would feel secure.

"You don't think I should go back, Tom?" she asked guiltily. "Daddy says he'll pay my fare."

It came as a shock to Tom, though the idea had crossed his mind that something of the kind might happen. "If that's the way you feel about it, I suppose you'd better, Elsie," he replied.

"But you wouldn't come with me."

"How can I come with you? You know I can't just walk out of the office for a couple of months."

"But you could get a job at home."

"And I told you a dozen times I don't want a job in America," he said angrily. Then, seeing the way it upset her, he changed his tone. "Look, if you stay here, feeling the way you do, you'll work yourself into a real illness. Anyway, sometime you'll have to go back on a visit, and this is as good an occasion as any."

"But how can I, without you?" she asked. "You'd only neglect yourself."

"I would not neglect myself."

"Would you stay at your mother's?"

"I would not stay at my mother's. This is my house, and I'm going to stop here."

Tom worried less about the effect Elsie's leaving would have on him than about what his family would say, particularly Annie, who never lost the chance of a crack at Elsie. "You let that girl walk on you, Tom Barry," she said. "One of these days she'll walk too hard." Then, of course, Tom walked on *her*, in the way that only a devoted brother can, but that was no relief to the feeling that something had come between Elsie and him and that he could do nothing about it. When he was driving Elsie to the liner, he knew that she felt the same, for she didn't break down until they came to a long grey bridge over an inlet of water, guarded by a lonely grey stone tower. She had once pointed it out to him as the first thing she had seen that represented

Ireland to her, and now he had the feeling that this was how she saw him—a battered old tower by a river mouth that was no longer of any importance to anyone but the seagulls.

She was away longer than she or anyone else had expected. First there was the wedding of an old school friend; then her mother's birthday; then the baby got ill. It was clear that she was enjoying herself immensely, but she wrote long and frequent letters, sent snapshots of herself and the baby, and—most important of all—had named the baby for Jerry Coakley. Clearly Elsie hadn't forgotten them. The Dorgan kids appeared on the road in clothes that had obviously been made in America, and whenever Tom met them he stopped to speak to them and give them the pennies he thought Elsie would have given them.

Occasionally Tom went to his mother's for supper, but otherwise he looked after himself. Nothing could persuade him that he was not a natural housekeeper, or that whatever his sisters could do he could not do just as well himself. Sometimes Jerry came and the two men took off their coats and tried to prepare a meal out of one of Elsie's cookbooks. "Steady, squad!" Tom would murmur as he wiped his hands before taking another peep at the book. "You never know when this might come in handy." But whether it was the result of Tom's supervision or Jerry's helplessness, the meal usually ended in a big burn-up, or a tasteless mess from which some essential ingredient seemed to be missing, and they laughed over it as they consoled themselves with bread and cheese and stout. "Elsie is right," Jerry would say, shaking his head regretfully. "We have problems, boy! We have problems!"

Elsie returned at last with trunks full of new clothes, a box of up-to-date kitchen stuff, and a new gaiety and energy. Every ten minutes Tom would make an excuse to tiptoe upstairs and take another look at his son. Then the Barrys arrived, and Elsie gave immediate offence by quoting Gesell and Spock. But Mrs. Barry didn't seem to mind as much as her daughters. By some extraordinary process of association, she had discovered a great similarity between Elsie and herself in the fact that she had married from the south side of the city into the north and had never got used to it. This delighted Elsie, who went about proclaiming that her mother-in-law and herself were both displaced persons.

The next year was a very happy one, and less trying on Elsie, because she had another woman to talk to, even if most of the time she didn't understand what her mother-in-law was telling her, and had the suspicion that her mother-in-law didn't understand her either. But then she got pregnant for the second time, and became restless and dissatisfied once more, though now it wasn't only with hospitals and doctors but with schools and school teachers as well. Tom and Jerry had impressed on her that the children were being turned into idiots, learning through the medium of a language they didn't understand—indeed, according to Tom, it was a language that nobody understood. What chance would the children have?

"Ah, I suppose the same chance as the rest of us, Elsie," said Jerry in his sly, mournful way.

"But you and Tom don't want chances, Jerry," she replied earnestly. "Neither of you has any ambition."

"Ah, you should look on the bright side of things.

Maybe with God's help they won't have any ambition either."

But this time it had gone beyond a joke. For days on end Tom was in a rage with her, and when he was angry he seemed to withdraw into himself like a snail into a shell.

Unable to get at him, Elsie grew hysterical. "It's all your damned obstinacy," she sobbed. "You don't do anything in this rotten hole, but you're too conceited to get out of it. Your family treat you as if you were God, and then you behave to me as if you were. God! God! God!" she screamed, and each time she punched him viciously with her fist, till suddenly the humour of their situation struck him and he went off into laughter.

After that he could only make his peace with her and make excuses for her leaving him again, but he knew that the excuses wouldn't impress his sisters. One evening when he went to see them, Annie caught him, as she usually did, when he was going out the front door, and he stood looking sidewise down the avenue.

"Are you letting Elsie go off to America again, Tom?" she asked.

"I don't know," Tom said, pulling his long nose with an air of affected indifference. "I can't very well stop her, can I?"

"Damn soon she'd be stopped if she hadn't the money," said Annie. "And you're going to let her take young Jerry?"

"Ah, how could I look after Jerry? Talk sense, can't you!"

"And I suppose we couldn't look after him either? We're not sufficiently well-read."

"Ah, the child should be with his own mother, Annie," Tom said impatiently.

"And where should his mother be? Ah, Tom Barry," she

added bitterly, "I told you what that one was, and she's not done with you yet. Are you sure she's going to bring him back?"

Then Tom exploded on her in his cold, savage way. "If you want to know, I am not," he said, and strode down the avenue with his head slightly bowed. Something about the cut of him as he passed under a street lamp almost broke Annie's heart. "The curse of God on that bitch!" she said when she returned to her mother in the kitchen.

"Is it Elsie?" her mother cried angrily. "How dare you talk of her like that!"

"He's letting her go to America again," said Annie.

"He's a good boy, and he's right to consider her feelings," said her mother anxiously. "I often thought myself I'd go back to the south side and not be ending my days in this misfortunate hole."

The months after Elsie's second departure were bitter ones for Tom. A house from which a woman is gone is bad enough, but one from which a child is gone is a dead house. Tom would wake in the middle of the night thinking he heard Jerry crying, and be half out of bed before he realised that Jerry was thousands of miles away. He did not continue his experiments with cooking and housekeeping. He ate at his mother's, spent most of his time at the Coakleys, and drank far too much. Like all inward-looking men he had a heavy hand on the bottle. Meanwhile Elsie wavered and procrastinated worse than before, setting dates, cancelling her passage, sometimes changing her mind within twenty-four hours. In his despondency Tom resigned himself to the idea that she wouldn't return at all, or at least persuaded himself that he had.

"Oh, she'll come back all right," Jerry said with a worried air. "The question is, will she stay back. . . . You don't mind me talking about it?" he asked.

"Indeed no. Why would I?"

"You know, Tom, I'd say ye had family enough to last ye another few years."

Tom didn't look up for a few moments, and when he did he smiled faintly. "You think it's that?"

"I'm not saying she knows it," Jerry added hastily. "There's nothing calculating about her, and she's crazy about you."

"I thought it was something that went with having the baby," Tom said thoughtfully. "Some sort of homing instinct."

"I wouldn't say so," said Jerry. "Not altogether. I think she feels that eventually she'll get you through the kids."

"She won't," Tom said bitterly.

"I know, sure, I know. But Elsie can't get used to the—the irremediable." The last word was so unlike Jerry that Tom felt he must have looked it up in a dictionary, and the absurdity of this made him feel very close to his old crony. "Tell me, Tom," Jerry added gently, "wouldn't you do it? I know it wouldn't be easy, but wouldn't you try it, even for a while, for Elsie's sake? "'Twould mean a hell of a lot to her."

"I'm too old, Jerry," Tom said so deliberately that Jerry knew it had been in his mind as well.

"Oh, I know, I know," Jerry repeated. "Even ten years ago I might have done it myself. It's like gaol. The time comes when you're happier in than out. And that's not the worst of it," he added bitterly. "The worst is when you pretend you like it."

It was a strange evening that neither of them ever forgot, sitting in that little house to which Elsie's absence seemed a rebuke, and listening to the wind from the harbor that touched the foot of the garden. They knew they belonged to a country whose youth was always escaping from it, out beyond that harbor, and that was middle-aged in all its attitudes and institutions. Of those that remained, a little handful lived with defeat and learned fortitude and humor and sweetness, and these were the things that Elsie, with her generous idealism, loved in them. But she couldn't pay the price. She wanted them where she belonged herself, among the victors.

A few weeks later Elsie was back; the house was full of life again, and that evening seemed only a bad dream. It was almost impossible to keep Jerry Og, as they called the elder child, away from Tom. He was still only a baby, and a spoiled one at that, but when Tom took him to the village Jerry Og thrust out his chest and took strides that were too big for him, like any small boy with a father he adored. Each day, he lay in wait for the postman and then took the post away to sort it for himself. He sorted it by the pictures on the stamps, and Elsie noted gleefully that he reserved all the pretty pictures for his father.

Nobody had remembered Jerry's good advice, even Jerry himself, and eighteen months later Elsie was pregnant again. Again their lives took the same pattern of unrest. But this time Elsie was even more distressed than Tom.

"I'm a curse to you," she said. "There's something wrong with me. I can't be natural."

"Oh, you're natural enough," Tom replied bitterly. "You married the wrong man, that's all."

"I didn't, I didn't!" she protested despairingly. "You can say anything else but that. If I believed that, I'd have nothing left, because I never cared for anyone but you. And in spite of what you think, I'm coming back," she went on, in tears. "I'm coming back if it kills me. God, I hate this country; I hate every goddam thing about it; I hate what it's done to you and Jerry. But I'm not going to let you go."

"You have no choice," Tom said patiently. "Jerry Og will have to go to school, and you can't be bringing him hither and over, even if you could afford it."

"Then, if that's what you feel, why don't you keep him?" she cried. "You know perfectly well you could stop me taking him with me if you wanted to. You wouldn't even have to bring me into court. I'll give him to you now. Isn't that proof enough that I'm coming back?"

"No, Elsie, it is not," Tom replied, measuring every word. "And I'm not going to bring you into court, either. I'm not going to take hostages to make sure my wife comes back to me."

And though Elsie continued to delude herself with the belief that she would return, she knew Tom was right. It would all appear different when she got home. The first return to Ireland had been hard, the second had seemed impossible. Yet, even in the black hours when she really considered the situation, she felt she could never resign herself to something that had been determined before she was born, and she deceived herself with the hope that Tom would change his mind and follow her. He must follow her. Even if he was prepared to abandon her he would never abandon Jerry Og.

And this, as Big Jerry could have told her, was where she

made her biggest mistake, because if Tom had done it at all it would have been for her. But Big Jerry had decided that the whole thing had gone beyond his power to help. He recognised the irremediable, all right, sometimes perhaps even before it became irremediable. But that, as he would have said himself, is where the ferryboat had left him.

Thanks to Elsie, the eldest of the Dorgans now has a job in Boston and in the course of years the rest of them will probably go there as well. Tom continues to live in his little bungalow beside the harbor. Annie is keeping house for him, which suits her fine, because Big Jerry's old mother continued to put his socks on for him a few years too long, and now Annie has only her brother to worship. To all appearances they are happy enough, as happiness goes in Cork. Jerry still calls, and the two men discuss the terrible state of the country. But in Tom's bedroom there are pictures of Elsie and the children, the third of whom he knows only through photographs, and, apart from that, nothing has changed since Elsie left it five years ago. It is a strange room, for one glance is enough to show that the man who sleeps there is still in love, and that everything that matters to him in the world is reflected there. And one day, if he comes by the dollars, he will probably go out and visit them all, but it is here he will return and here, no doubt, he will die.

The Man Who Stepped on His Soul

Seán Mac Mathúna

THERE IS A BEACH in Kerry, long and straight as a knife, clean as a chalice, and the first men that gazed upon it sighed, and called it Lonely Banna Strand. Press a shell to your ear and hear its loneliness, windswept and timeless down by an endless sea. Far out where all is still, sunlight drops through the tall green gloom of the ocean, but inshore land and wave commemorate each other with dry satisfying sand. And when the wind blows, it tosses seagulls far inland beyond the trees, beyond the fields, beyond the hills; or wilder still, it funnels sand through the keyholes of distant homes, and the surf booms out across the county reminding the old of forgotten things, haunting the

SEÁN MAC MATHÚNA (1936–) was born in Tralee. Mac Mathúna's short stories have been published in English in *The Irish Times*, *The Irish Press* and in Irish in such publications as *Comhar*. His collection of short stories *Ding* (1983) established Mac Mathúna as a talented short story writer. *The Atheist and Other Stories* (1987), confirmed his reputation as a writer of some importance. In 1999 his second collection of short stories, *Banana*, was published. *Banana* won the Gradam Uí Shúilleabháin/Irish Book of the Year 1999.

young with the triumph of days to come. But its fury is the fury of mindless things and in such fury only do we find the stillness of true peace.

It wasn't for nothing it was called Lonely Banna Strand, said Tom Mullins to himself, as he cycled from his monastery westwards to the sea. He watched the fuzzy line of sandhills hop, step, and jump southward to the Sliabh Mish mountains. But why do the people of Kerry now call it Banna Beach? They had already lost one language without a trace of culture shock. They would gladly lose another if they got half a chance. The word *strand* stood for loneliness and the washed vacancy of ocean margins; *beach* on the other hand brought to mind barbecues, broken bottles and unwanted human commotion. A full year now he had been in the Black Monastery of Doon, and his opinion of Kerry people had grown thin. Culture had no meaning for them, nothing worried them except pub closing times, and where was the crack. In a group they reminded him of empty Coke bottles rattling together.

These spiteful observations eased the rheumatic hip enough for him to dismount and walk a little. It was the first few days of April and there wasn't enough snow on Sliabh Mish to satisfy a robin on a Christmas postcard. It was a day as frail as the spindrift, and although cold, there was enough sunlight to tempt one to be adventurous with clothes. He loosened his Roman collar with a finger.

It was going to be a great geographical day, for geographer he was at heart and thus coveted nature's wilderness. Today, Banna Strand would be his Gobi Desert, tomorrow the bog of Lyracrumpane would be his Okavango Swamps.

He was a man who enjoyed the mystical unity of rock, tree and river, and though the geography of Ireland pleased him, it was too equable and lacked the passion of the extreme. That was why he was so devoted to all those *National Geographic*s that were piled under his bed. Once a month Season Finlay, the Brother Superior, would toss the yellow magazine on the table in front of Mullins, always when there was company about. He had done it yesterday.

"I see the subscription is up again," his tone a mixture of censure and threat.

"Beauty never comes cheap," Mullins had replied.

"There's a geographical magazine produced in England which is much cheaper and more scientific, I believe," the Superior offered.

"It's not for the science that I read it."

"What for then?" Finlay's face grew a disfiguring leer and his fat eyes winked little signals at the rest of the group.

Mullins ignored the spite. After all, had he not taken a vow of humility, which had to earn its keep. He could hardly tell the company that the full-color magazine primed his youthful soul for journeys to the bottom of the Marianas Trench, or maybe in a balloon all the way to La Paz. And of late, as the grey winds of middle age blew all about him all the more, he had taken refuge in long-lining off the Grand Banks, or on cold days he accompanied Van der Post to the centre of the Kalahari Desert.

"You must have quite a lot gathered by now," added the Superior.

"Yes—quite a lot."

He had in fact 323 *National Geographic*s to be exact under his bed. There was room only for 120 more. By that time

he would be fifty years of age. It was as good a way as any
for marking time on this earth, being informed regularly
by post that another month had passed.

"Why do you keep them? Why not give them to the
poor and the needy?" asked Finlay.

"I like to reread them from time to time," he answered.
Finlay had drawn himself up to his full height and had said
with a smile, "I have never in my life had to reread a book,"
and he walked away through the refectory.

Mullins left the tar road, and, leaving his bike against a
rotting boat, made his way out through the dunes, silently
like an actor through the wings out onto a sunlit stage. One
glance up and down was enough—tabula rasa—Banna
Strand was all his, not a footprint in sight. Seeing other
people's footprints on his strand was as distasteful as reading other people's letters.

Well, he was going to have a fine Gobi-Desert day. He
felt as joyous as Marco Polo did the first day he set foot in
it. Mullins eyed the imposing Altai mountains to the east,
then took another hearing from the Nan Shan mountains to
the south. You had to do that sort of thing for you could get
lost easily in a desert—like the sea—and for that reason
men who loved the deserts also loved the sea. With his shoe
he nudged the sand. Dinosaur eggs had been discovered here
once. But he wouldn't dig for them today. He looked about
for his favourite Gobi mammal, the Mongolian wild ass. Not
a sign. Pity—for it was great to watch them doing 45 miles
per hour in and out of the dunes. Down he strolled through
the middle of his desert, whistling a gay tune for there are
great acoustics in a desert. The people of the world did not
understand their deserts, especially geographers, who quite

frequently left them as blank spaces on their maps, simply because they lacked roads and towns and data on wheat production. No, deserts were cosy corners in Space, in Time, where man could empty his mind of spite, and listen to it trickle through the silent dunes for ever.

He came to a stream. Was it the Orhon or the Nank Fat? It didn't matter. He took off his shoes and stockings and rolled up his trousers. With a shoe in each hand, he dashed across the stream, but it was so numbing he almost fell in the middle. He raced out to the other side and danced on the lukewarm sand. Then he dried himself with a large white handkerchief. Suddenly he looked up—the Gobi had vanished.

He strolled to the water's edge, but had to retreat from the waves' long fetch. There was something very satisfying in the way they pounded the strand, the way they hung for a second like walls of glass with bits of seaweed trapped in them before they shattered to smithereens for ever; but spindrift began to fly and he stuck to the centre of the strand where the sand was just right for footprints. Crunch—crunch—crunch, his black polished shoes bit the sand setting up a tempo that had satisfied man since the beginning of time. He glanced behind him as he walked on and he saw the way his footprints careered about. They followed him—they were loyal. He stopped. They were about the only thing that would ever follow him in this life, each print punctuating his aloneness. But footprints would never keep the wind off your back. It must be wonderful to have a family, to have children— they'd warm your back, especially that little patch between the shoulder blades. Ah, but was he not one of the Cold

Backs of the Monastery of Doon. He walked on and pondered good humoredly if they had sent him to Doon because it rhymed with doom.

But all of this was not satisfactory. Geography had escaped—introversion had arrived. Going in search of self was useless because self in its own good time came after you with a vengeance. Suddenly he saw something move. The landscape was changing, he was no longer alone. Somebody was heading down the strand towards him, spoiling things for him. He was niggardly about his wildernesses. He was about to turn for home when something about the approaching person made him pause. It was a woman, her hands waving at him as she stumbled along the base of the dunes. She fell and did not get up. Brother Mullins settled his hat on his head and headed off at a trot towards her. When he came up to her she was on her hands and knees gasping for breath, her blonde hair caging her face to the ground.

"Are you alright, something wrong?"

She raised her head still gasping, she was about thirty-five. She pointed back along the dunes.

"My husband," she gasped, "he's dying back there, he keeps shouting for a priest, will you go back to him, Father, I can't budge another step."

She was American, he was sure of that. And he wasn't budging either, he was doubly sure of that.

"I regret to inform you, Madam, that I am not a priest."

His tone was quite sharp—sharpness was respected. Woe to the meek—they did not inherit the earth. She looked open-mouthed at him.

"Aren't you a clergyman?"

"It's not a term I use. I am, madam, a member of the order of Christian Brothers. Brothers do not have confessional faculties. If you require a priest you will get one in the church of Tineel, some distance from here."

"I don't give a damn what you are. Go back to my husband please, please, he's dying, anybody will do." He was about to point out to her that he wasn't anybody either, but the helplessness, the pleading and the fear made him cancel his words.

"OK," he said, and he set off along her set of prints without adding what was on the tip of his tongue—as long as there's no more of this priest business. For Mullins had a fierce pride and he was tired of being mistaken by people everywhere for a priest; brothers dressed exactly the same, except that their Roman collars were half an inch thinner than priests'. When people discovered their mistake they had to revise their opinion of you—and it was in this revision that all the damage was done right before your eyes. You had to stop them fast to reduce the extent of the revision.

"I am not a priest, I'm only a brother." Only—may God deliver only the good. And then they said, "Ah well, sure a brother is almost as good as a priest." That *almost* was reductive, very. People couldn't cope with the pressure of readjustment. "Oh well, sure everybody has to be something." It was enough to make one want to join the Franciscans. Priests—he hated their seed and breed.

The woman was struggling along behind him.

"How about a doctor?" he shouted back.

"Too late," she gasped, "he's on a drug, Lysembuthol, if that doesn't work forget it."

They pressed on. His left ear was exposed to the sea

breeze and his earhole filled with sand. But his obsession with priests wouldn't let him alone. There had been that occasion in Salthill years ago when two priests in a car had drawn up at the kerb and said "Would you like a lift, Father?" He had unwound his scarf and shown them his collar. "Well would you like a lift anyway?" He had refused with a smile. As their car had pulled away he had envied them their worldliness, their car, their freedom, the fact that they didn't have a vow of poverty as he had. No, he didn't hate priests, it was just that they reminded him that he may have followed the wrong track in life.

Talking about tracks, they were running out of them in the dunes—lost. He waited and watched her try to climb a steep path up to him. She failed and looked helplessly at him. He took her hand and he instantly liked the sensation of her cold fingers being warmed in his fist. So much so he was slow to relinquish it.

"I'm lost," she said.

"Must be this way," he said, and they trotted off again.

Suddenly they were there; a perfect sandy crater and a man of about fifty prostrate, gasping, eyes staring at the clouds that flung their shadows recklessly at the dunes. His blue cheeks matched the blue of his shirt. A red polka-dot bow tie moved to the rhythm of his gasping, flecks of foam clinging to a small mustache. This man's number is up, Mullins said to himself as he went on one knee beside him. The man tried to raise himself on his elbow and say something, but the woman pressed him back gently, placing her handbag under his head.

"Take it easy Sean, everything is going to be alright, we have got ourselves some help."

She loosened his shirt and dusted the sand from it. Mullins had to make room for her and as he did his shadow fell across the man's face, and as it did the man's eyes fastened on the clerical collar.

"Father," he gasped, "I'm bunched—must make my confession fast. Haven't been a good boy you know, Mass, Communion and that sort of thing."

His hand clawed at Mullins' coat for assurance that deathbed confessions would put his soul in the black again.

"I regret very much, my good man, that I'm not in a position to hear your confession or give you absolution." Mullins felt satisfaction in the words which were delivered with the tiniest bit of spite for good measure; that would teach him not to call him Father.

"Still I appreciate your condition and I would very much like to—"

The man grabbed him by the lapel and almost pulled him down on top of him.

"For God's sake, you don't have to be a bishop—it's only a piddling confession—a bit of a blessing and everything is just bully, real bully, right?"

"Right," said Mullins instinctively, because he couldn't refuse the pleading in the woman's eyes, and he didn't like violence either.

No sooner had he said the word than the man was off cutting through his confession, "Bless me, Father, for I have sinned," followed by a rattle of familiar clichés.

Mullins almost broke out in a sweat. This was undoubtedly the worst position he had ever been in.

"I killed somebody."

The man waited for a reaction from the priest. Mullins

stared in fright at him, this was it, he was going to get up and run, he wasn't getting involved in that sort of thing.

"In the Arctic," said the man.

The word *Arctic* made Mullins pause.

"I never touched the creature but I still killed him—I'll tell you about it."

Mullins nodded.

"We were off Baffin Island in a big trawler out of Halifax, hunting halibut, but we were too far north and too close to Greenland. The winter was closing in and that damned williwaw was blowing. But we were too greedy. Instead of heading south and running, we edged north. Strike halibut and you can spend a couple of months in Mexico. But the weather hardened."

"How far north were you? Melville?"

The man looked strangely at Mullins.

"No," he said, about 75° North, near a peninsula called Urumsuak, I think."

Mullins had forgotten the confession—now he was turning pages of the frozen North with full color photography.

"Well, we struck halibut alright, but the rigging froze and we went top heavy and the strain blew the bloody boiler on us. Myself and four others barely made it to the Greenland coast—ice everywhere. We knew our number was up but still we pressed along the edge of the pack."

"What temperature?"

The man squinted oddly.

"Easily forty below."

"That's celsius of course."

The man's brow puckered, for he didn't know that he was now a talking *National Geographic.*

"There was no sun at noon, just a glimmer enough to

see the polar bear. That scared us—we had no gun. That's when you know how yellow you are.

Petrov, the Russian, had no gloves. His fingers turned to charcoal. He was a goner."

"I know," said Mullins—see *National Geographic* P.864, No. 6, Vol. CXIV.

"We watched his soul leak out of his eyes and his breath go spare, as we left him on a hunk of ice. Some other fella fell into a lead and never surfaced. Shortly after that we came on a small Eskimo igloo. We could have danced. He was an old hunter and we all huddled in. It was warm, it was shelter. But he had a child about a year old wrapped in a bearskin. Never could figure out how the child got there. These old Eskimos are as odd as hell, often take off for a week with a child for company. Well there was very little light the next day either but towards evening we saw rigging lights out in the bay. This must have been the last trawler on the coast. It was our last chance or we'd go like Petrov. Well, the Eskimo had this fiberglass boat—they don't have kayaks anymore— but he wouldn't take us out. Schumacher, the mate, said we were due for a black blizzard and the trawler would skip before it. But the Eskimo wouldn't budge—he kept pointing at the little child. He refused money. Schumacher began to shout. The Eskimo got worried and pulled an old gun on us—there was a struggle, a shot, and the old guy dropped."

"Dead?"

"Like a stone."

He drew two deep breaths, his chest pumping up and down. "You see the poor old devil felt the child would die if anything happened to himself. Anyway Eskimos don't trust whites."

"I see their point."

"Anyway, that was an accident. Outside the igloo Schumacher said fog was coming. Up there, fog is the angel of death. We cut the heels off each other racing for the boat. We paddled like mad to the trawler. About fifty yards out we heard the child cry. We had forgotten, we stopped paddling, then we heard it again. Slowly and silently we paddled on and the wail of that child never left the stern of the boat. The trawler captain was outraged when he saw us. He had no room for us but he had no choice. When I mentioned the child to him he almost stabbed me with the marlinspike."

He settled himself on the sand again, eyes as bloodshot as the setting sun.

"The cry, Father, of that child has followed me down the years." He paused. "And that's about it, I killed a child, that's my confession." A note of self-pity came into his words. "I've paid for it I tell you, year after year of bad luck, bad health, I've been dogged, I've paid for it in this life, I'm damned if I'm going to pay for it also in the next. Now be a good man and tell me you understand."

Mullins didn't understand at all. His mind was a big windy space, and if the things that should be in his mind were there, it's not in Banna he'd be now, but living with the gauchos of the Pampas, or exploring the headwaters of the Rio Negro. But there was just this space there and the sea breeze whistling through.

"I suppose," Mullins said, "that the child didn't last too long."

"No, a couple of days, I'd say, hunger and cold."

"Tell me, did you think of blocking up the entrance?"

"No," the man looked startled.

"Anything could have got in then."

The man held his gaze for a moment, then his head fell back again.

"Christ!" was all he said.

"Look," said Mullins, "what you did was not noble but the circumstances are unusual. You are contrite and as you say you have suffered. God, any God, would understand. You are forgiven, I'm sure."

"Fine, Father, fine, but just to be on the safe side give me absolution."

"That's something I can't do for you, son."

"Why not?"

"I'm not a priest."

"You're not a priest!" He was turning an ugly purple again.

"Yes, you see I'm a Christian Brother." He was up on one elbow again, the line of his mouth twisted into an S hook.

"Jesus, he's only a Brother."

He looked about him at the world with eyes that would drive nails into the wall. He fell back again on the sand.

"What a joke, confessed to a Brother, that's it then, my tune is played, the dance is over."

The woman moved in from her discreet distance, concern in her voice.

"Take it easy Sean, it doesn't matter one way or the other."

"Look," said Mullins in desperation, "I'll do something which is every bit as good as absolution."

"What's that?"

"The Act of Contrition. Repeat after me, Oh my God, I'm heartily sorry for having offended thee—."

The man was up like a shot.

"You can shove your contrition up your ass. I know what this is now." He was screaming. "This is vengeance planned by God. Oh God, you're a cute hoor, all these years you were waiting to get me. And now you have me shanghaied in Banna, miles from nowhere and no absolution. You left me without children, that wasn't enough, now you want me to burn for eternity."

His face constricted and he fell back. His wife moved fast.

"Attack, attack," she hissed, "he's got another attack." She felt his pulse. "Nothing," she said.

She placed her ear over his heart, her blonde hair pouring over his blue shirt. Nice color scheme, Mullins thought. The wind had gathered a drop at the tip of his nose, and he felt it would be inopportune to wipe it.

"Can you do mouth-to-mouth?" She noticed the disgust on his face. "OK," she said, "strike him on the chest with your fist when I tell you."

Mullins prepared himself over the body and rolled up his sleeve. The hair covered the head and chest again. Mullins was ashamed that he did not feel an ounce of pity, his own predicament had cancelled it.

"Now!"

Mullins gave the chest a small punch.

"Harder!"

He punched him harder again and again, so much that it hurt his hand.

"Anything doing?" he asked.

She shook her head. They both knew he was dead, heading down through the Milky Way, going God knows where. Still they kept it up, blow, punch, blow, punch. From time to time sand pelted them from the crests of the dunes, but she brushed every grain off the shirt. She was pale, he noticed, but calm, and those blue eyes that couldn't have hidden a thought. Unsly eyes were rare. Still, he didn't want her looking straight at him, for she gave him the flutters and he wanted to keep it dark.

"He's gone," she said simply, sitting back on her heels.

"Maybe we should get a doctor."

"He's gone, I said, I'm a nurse."

"Maybe we should get a priest."

"Is he going to make him sit up and walk?"

He didn't reply—in the circumstances it was a ridiculous suggestion.

"I need to close his eyes, have you got some coins?"

He fished and gave her two pennies. She did it with care, pulling down the blinds on the eye-shaped world of Sean somebody, who now looked up at the clouds with a harp and hen with her chicks.

"These are awfully big pennies," she said.

"Next month we are going decimal and they will be much smaller."

Yes, everything he said was ridiculous. "Shouldn't we do something?" he offered.

"Like what?"

"I don't know."

She sighed. "I knew this was going to happen. It was only a question of where." She looked about her. "I suppose this is as good as any, the sea, the sand, the cleanliness of it all." Her eyes misted over and a tear squeezed out of an eye. "What was all that about a while ago?"

"What?"

"The anger, the fear."

"That, madam, was the fear of God."

She pursed her lips and nodded. "Fear and terror. Any trace of love in this land?" She took the dead man's hand in hers and twirled the ring on his finger, then pressed it to her cheek. "Fifteen years married and all that time he gave me respect, good nature, humor, yeah, heart and soul. But three weeks ago we landed in Ireland—his home-land—and he changes overnight—sort of a cloud came down on him—worried about his mother, his family, his childhood. We visited all those broken-down cabins on that mountain there," she indicated Sliabh Mish, "it was like leading a frightened child through the dark. I'm sure there must also be love in this land."

Mullins felt trapped again, trapped in a drama without a script. Why ask me about love, lady, love is a snow-capped mountain in the distance that everybody has climbed but me, love is a word you use to win an argument, to lose an argument, to win someone, to lose someone, love was a word to give yourself stature or to diminish someone else, it was the most common word in the spiri-tual writings of Rodriguez, all over Sunday sermons, evening devotions, nightly prayers—love is luck, some-thing other people have, love was as common as ghosts—he had seen neither.

She was shivering. He took off his black overcoat and draped it around her shoulders.

"You don't have to do that, now you'll be cold."

He was but he didn't care.

"Where are you going now?" he asked.

"Back to the Napa Valley, California, with Sean. Where will you go?"

"Back to the monastery, Vespers. They're prayers."

"It must be lonely in a monastery."

Sure, it was, so lonely sometimes he bit into his prayer book. Teeth marks everywhere.

"No, not really," he said, "there is great solace in prayer." Liar, you might as well be reciting eeny, meeny, miny, mo. Tell her now, tell her the truth, you've never told anyone. Think of the relief. Sigh, and say it, be a man.

"It is refreshing to hear that," she said. "I'm glad that human nature has so many resources. What do they call you, your name I mean?"

Tom, you fool, say Tom. To hear her say Tom once would be better than all the yellow rubbish you have under the bed, out with it.

"Brother is the correct form of address."

"Brother." She said it matter-of-factly.

It sounded like two sods falling on his coffin. There was a long silence between them. She looked so small in his overcoat, the weak evening sun making candlelight dance in her eyes.

"I better go for an ambulance then."

She nodded. "What about your coat?"

"Never mind about that," he said, climbing the dune. Then he paused. "I'm sorry about all this, I wish I could have done what he wanted."

"It's better to be honest," were her last words.

Then he was racing down the other side of the dune, and then through the others until finally he hit the strand, the long windy strand. The spindrift was flying inland like flock as he came upon his footprints and hers. Damn it, he hadn't even the courtesy to ask her her name. He was freezing without his coat. He stopped and looked about the blue and gold landscape.

"Honest she said," he almost roared. "I'm not honest, I can pretend the Gobi but I can't pretend to be a priest. But I pretend to be serene when I am the loneliest man in the whole world. Sweet Christ, I'm lonelier than Lonely Banna Strand."

He crunched ahead. The *National Geographic*s would have to go. His mind was going technicolor and soft. He might as well yield to the shadows of the grey years that marched towards him like the dunes.

Away to the south, mountains purpled out of sight into the mists of Dingle. To the east the Stacks reared up saying thou shalt not pass. To the west was an endless sea, haughty in its wild commotion. To the north there would be something else, but he would not look back for was he not Tom Mullins, the man who stepped on his soul. He really didn't see anything, for now, the world was only as wide as a woman's face, or as narrow as the cold spot between the shoulder blades, and all he knew of Banna was the booming of the waves which would follow him all the way to the gates of the monastery. And thus the coldness grew within.

A Scandalous Woman

Edna O'Brien

EVERYONE IN OUR VILLAGE was unique, and one or two of the girls were beautiful. There were others before and after, but it was with Eily I was connected. Sometimes one finds oneself in the swim, one is wanted, one is favored, one is privy, one is caught up in another's destiny that is far more exciting than one's own.

Hers was the face of a madonna. She had brown hair, a great crop of it, fair skin, and eyes that were as big and as

EDNA O'BRIEN (1930–) was born in Tuamgraney, County Clare, in 1930. O'Brien published her first book, *The Country Girls,* in 1960. *The Country Girls* was the first part of a trilogy of novels (later collected as *The Country Girls Trilogy*), which included *The Lonely Girl* (1962) and *Girls in Their Married Bliss* (1964). O'Brien has received numerous awards for her works, including the Kingsley Amis Award in 1962, and the Los Angeles Times Book Prize in 1990 for *Lantern Slides*. Her short stories include *The Love Object & Other Stories* (1968), *A Scandalous Woman and Other Stories* (1974), *Mrs Reinhardt and Other Stories* (1978), and *A Fanatic Heart: Selected Stories* (1984). In 2006 Edna O' Brien was appointed professor of English Literature at University College Dublin.

soft and as transparent as ripe gooseberries. She was always a little out of breath and gasped when one approached, then embraced and said, "Darling." That was when we met in secret. In front of her parents and others she was somewhat stubborn and withdrawn, and there was a story that when young she always lived under the table to escape her father's thrashings. For one Advent she thought of being a nun, but that fizzled out and her chief interests became clothes and needlework. She helped on the farm and used not to be let out much in the summer, because of all the extra work. She loved the main road with the cars and the bicycles and the buses, and had no interest at all in the sidecar that her parents used for conveyance. She would work like a horse to get to the main road before dark to see the passersby. She was swift as a colt. My father never stopped praising this quality in her and put it down to muscle. It was well known that Eily and her family hid their shoes in a hedge near the road, so that they would have clean footwear when they went to Mass, or to market, or, later on, in Eily's case, to the dress dance.

The dress dance in aid of the new mosaic altar marked her debut. She wore a georgette dress and court shoes threaded with silver and gold. The dress had come from America long before but had been restyled by Eily, and during the week before the dance she was never to be seen without a bunch of pins in her mouth as she tried out some different fitting. Peter the Master, one of the local tyrants, stood inside the door with two or three of his cronies, both to count the money and to survey the couples and comment on their clumsiness or on their dancing "technique." When Eily arrived in her tweed coat and said, "Evening, gentlemen," no one passed any remark, but the moment she slipped off the coat and the transparency of the georgette plus her naked shoulders were revealed, Peter the Master spat into the palm of his hand and said didn't she strip a fine woman.

The locals were mesmerized. She was not off the floor once, and the more she danced, the more fetching she became, and was saying "ooh" and "aah" as her partners spun her round and round. Eventually one of the ladies in charge of the supper had to take her into the supper room and fan her with a bit of cardboard. I was let to look in the window, admiring the couples and the hanging streamers and the very handsome men in the orchestra with their sideburns and striped suits. Then in the supper room, where I had stolen to, Eily confided to me that something out of this world had taken place. Almost immediately after, she was brought home by her sister, Nuala.

Eily and Nuala always quarreled—issues such as who would milk, or who would separate the milk, or who would draw water from the well, or who would churn, or who would bake bread. Usually Eily got the lighter tasks, because of her breathlessness and her accomplishments with the needle. She was wonderful at knitting and could copy any stitch just from seeing it in a magazine or in a knitting pattern. I used to go over there to play, and though they were older than me, they used to beg me to come and bribe me with empty spools or scraps of cloth for my dolls. Sometimes we played hide-and-seek, sometimes we played families and gave ourselves posh names and posh jobs, and we used to paint each other with the dye from plants or blue bags and treat one another's faces as if they were palettes, and then laugh and marvel at the blues and indigos and pretend to be natives and do hula-hula and eat dock leaves.

Nuala was happiest when someone was upset, and almost always she trumped for playing hospital. She was doctor and Eily was nurse. Nuala liked to operate with a big black carving knife, and long before she commenced, she gloated over the method and over what tumors she was going to remove. She used to say that there would be nothing but a shell by the time she had finished, and that one wouldn't be able to have babies or women's complaints ever. She had names for the female parts of one, Susies for the breasts, Florries for the stomach, and Matilda for lower down. She would sharpen and resharpen the knife on the steps, order Eily to get the hot water, the soap, to sterilize the utensils and to have to hand a big winding sheet.

Eily also had to don an apron, a white apron that formerly she had worn at cookery classes. The kettle always took an age to boil on the open hearth, and very often Nuala threw sugar on it to encourage the flame. The two doors would be wide open, a bucket against one and a stone to the other. Nuala would be sharpening the knife and humming "Waltzing Matilda," the birds would almost always be singing or chirruping, the dogs would be outside on their hindquarters, snapping at flies, and I would be lying on the kitchen table, terrified and in a state of undress. Now and then, when I caught Eily's eye, she would raise hers to heaven as much as to say, "you poor little mite," but she never contradicted Nuala or disobeyed orders. Nuala would don her mask. It was a bright-red papier-mâché mask that had been in the house from the time when some mummers came on the Day of the Wren, got bitten by the dog, and lost some of their regalia, including the mask and a legging. Before she commenced, she let out a few dry, knowing coughs, exactly imitating the doctor's dry, knowing coughs. I shall never stop remembering those last few seconds as she snapped the elastic band around the back of her head and said to Eily, "All set, Nurse?"

For some reason I always looked upward and backward and therefore could see the dresser upside down, and the contents of it. There was a whole row of jugs, mostly white jugs with sepia designs of corn, or cattle, or a couple toiling in the fields. The jugs hung on hooks at the edge of the dresser, and behind them were the plates with ripe pears painted in the center of each one. But most beautiful of all were the little dessert dishes of carnival glass, with their orange tints and their scalloped edges. I used to say goodbye to them, and then it would be time to close eyes before the ordeal.

She never called it an operation, just an "op," the same as the doctor did. I would feel the point of the knife like the point of a compass going around my scarcely formed breasts. My bodice would not be removed, just lifted up. She would comment on what she saw and say, "Interesting," or "Quite," or "Oh, dearie me," as the case may be, and then when she got at the stomach she would always say, "Tut tut tut," and "What nasty business have we got here." She would list the unwholesome things I had been eating, such as sherbet or rainbow toffees, hit my stomach with the flat of the knife, and order two spoons of turpentine and three spoons of castor oil before commencing. These potions had then to be downed. Meanwhile, Eily, as the considerate nurse, would be mopping the doctor's brow and handing extra implements such as sugar tongs, spoon, or fork. The spoon was to flatten the tongue and make the patient say "Aah." Scabs or cuts would be regarded as nasty devils, and elastic marks as a sign of iniquity. I would also have to make a general confession. I used to lie there praying that their mother would come home unexpectedly. It was always a Tuesday, the day their mother went to the market to sell things, to buy commodities, and to draw her husband's pension. I used to wait for a sound from the dogs. They were vicious dogs and bit everyone except their owners, and on my arrival there I used to have to yell for Eily to come out and escort me past them.

All in all, it was a woeful event, but still I went each Tuesday on the way home from school, and by the time their mother returned, all would be over and I would be sitting demurely by the fire, waiting to be offered a shop biscuit, which of course at first I made a great pretense of refusing.

Eily always conveyed me down the first field as far as the white gate, and though the dogs snarled and showed their teeth, they never tried biting once I was leaving. One evening, though it was nearly milking time, she came farther, and I thought it was to gather a few hazelnuts, because there was a little tree between our boundary and theirs that was laden with them. You had only to shake the tree for the nuts to come tumbling down, and you had only to sit on the nearby wall, take one of the loose stones, and crack away to your heart's content. They were just ripe, and they tasted young and clean, and helped as well to get all fur off the backs of the teeth. So we sat on the wall, but Eily did not reach up and draw a branch and therefore a shower of nuts down. Instead, she asked me what I thought of Romeo. He was a new bank clerk, a Protestant, and to me a right toff in his plus fours with his white sports bicycle. The bicycle had a dynamo attached, so that he was never without lights. He rode the bicycle with his body hunched forward, so that as she mentioned him I could see his snout and his lock of falling hair coming toward me on the road. He also distinguished himself by riding the bicycle into shops or hallways. In fact, he was scarcely ever off it. It seems he had danced with her the night she wore the green georgette, and next day left a note in the hedge where she and her family kept their shoes. She said it was the grace of God that she had gone there first thing that morning, otherwise the note might have come into someone else's hand. He had made an assignation for the following Sunday, and she did not know how she was going to get out of her house and under what excuse. At least Nuala was gone, back to Technical School, where she was learning to be a domestic-economy instructor, and my sisters had returned to the convent, so that we were able to hatch it without the bother of them eavesdropping on us. I said yes, I would be her accomplice, without knowing what I was letting myself in for. On Sunday I told my parents that I was going with Eily to visit a cousin of theirs in the hospital, and she in turn told her parents that we were visiting a cousin of mine. We met at the white gate and both of us were peppering. She had an old black dirndl skirt which she slipped out of; underneath was her cerise dress with the slits at the side. It was a most compromising garment. She wore a brooch at the bosom. Her mother's brooch, a plain flat gold pin with a little star in the center that shone feverishly. She took out her little gold flapjack and proceeded to dab powder on. She removed the little muslin cover, made me hold it delicately while she dipped into the powder proper. It was ocher stuff and completely wrecked her complexion. Then she applied lipstick, wet her kiss curl, and made me kneel down in the field and promise never ever to spill.

We went toward the hospital, but instead of going up that dark cedar-lined avenue, we crossed over a field, nearly drowning ourselves in the swamp, and permanently stooping so as not to be sighted. I said we were like soldiers in a war and she said we should have worn green or brown as camouflage. Her shapely bottom, bobbing up and down, could easily have been spotted by anyone going along the road. When we got to the thick of the woods, Romeo was there. He looked very indifferent, his face forward, his head almost as low as the handlebars of the bicycle, and he surveyed us carefully as we approached. Then he let out a couple of whistles to let her know how welcome she was. She stood beside him, and I faced them, and we all remarked what a fine evening it was. I could hardly believe my eyes when I saw his hand go around her waist, and then her dress crumpled as it was being raised up from the back, and though the two of them stood perfectly still, they were both looking at each other intently and making signals with their lips. Her dress was above the back of her knees. Eily began to get very flushed and he studied her face most carefully, asking if it was nice, nice. I was told by him to run along: "Run along, Junior" was what he said. I went and adhered to the bark of a tree, eyes closed, fists closed, and every bit of me in a clinch. Not long after, Eily hollered, and on the way home and walking very smartly, she and I discussed growing pains and she said there were no such things but that it was all rheumatism.

So it continued Sunday after Sunday, with one holy day, Ascension Thursday, thrown in. We got wizard in our excuses—once it was to practice with the school choir, another time it was to teach the younger children how to receive Holy Communion, and once—this was our riskiest ploy—it was to get gooseberries from an old crank called Miss MacNamara. That proved to be dangerous, because both our mothers were hoping for some, either for eating or for stewing, and we had to say that Miss MacNamara was not home, whereupon they said weren't the bushes there anyhow with the gooseberries hanging off. For a moment I imagined that I had actually been there, in the little choked garden with moldy bushes, weighed down with the big hairy gooseberries that were soft to the touch and that burst when you bit into them. We used to pray on the way home, say prayers and ejaculations, and very often when we leaned against the grass bank while Eily donned her old skirt and her old canvas shoes, we said one or another of the Mysteries of the Rosary. She had new shoes that were slippers really and that her mother had not seen. They were olive green and she bought them from a gypsy woman in return for a tablecloth of her mother's that she had stolen. It was a special

cloth that had been sent all the way from Australia by a
nun. She was a thief as well. One day all these sins would
have to be reckoned with. I used to shudder at night when
I went over the number of commandments we were both
breaking, but I grieved more on her behalf, because she was
breaking the worst one of all in those embraces and trans-
actions with him. She never discussed him except to say
that his middle name was Jack.

During those weeks my mother used to say I was pale
and why wasn't I eating and why did I gargle so often with
salt and water. These were forms of atonement to God.
Even seeing Eily on Tuesdays was no longer the source of
delight that it used to be. I was racked. I used to say, "Is
this a dagger which I see before me," and recalled all the
queer people around who had visions and suffered from
delusions. The same would be our cruel cup. She flared up.
"Marry! did I or did I not love her?" Of course I loved her
and would hang for her, but she was asking me to do the
two hardest things on earth—to disobey God and my own
mother. Often she took huff, swore that she would get
someone else—usually Una, my greatest rival—to play
gooseberry for her and be her dogsbody in her whole secret
life. But then she would make up and be waiting for me on
the road as I came from school, and we would climb in over
the wall that led to their fields, and we would link and discuss the possible excuse for the following Sunday. Once,
she suggested wearing the green georgette, and even I, who
also lacked restraint in matters of dress, thought it would
draw untoward attention to her, since it was a dance dress
and since as Peter the Master had said, she looked stripped
in it. I said Mrs. Bolan would smell a rat. Mrs. Bolan was

one of the many women who were always prowling and turning up at graveyards or in the slate quarry to see if there were courting couples. She always said she was looking for stray turkeys or turkey eggs, but in fact she had no fowl, and was known to tell tales that were calumnious; as a result, one temporary schoolteacher had to leave the neighborhood, do a flit in the night, and did not even have time to get her shoes back from the cobbler's. But Eily said that we would never be found out, that the god Cupid was on our side, and while I was with her I believed it.

I had a surprise a few evenings later. Eily was lying in wait for me on the way home from school. She peeped up over the wall, said "Yoo-hoo," and then darted down again. I climbed over. She was wearing nothing under her dress, since it was such a scorching day. We walked for a bit, then we flopped down against a cock of hay, the last one in the field, as the twenty-three other cocks had been brought in the day before. It looked a bit silly and was there only because of an accident: the mare had bolted, broken away from the hay cart, and nearly strangled the driver, who was himself an idiot and whose chin was permanently smeared with spittle. She said to close my eyes, open my hands, and see what God would give me. There are moments in life when the pleasure is more than one can bear, and one descends willy-nilly into a wild tunnel of flounder and vertigo. It happens on swing boats and chairoplanes, it happens maybe at waterfalls, it is said to happen to some when they fall in love, but it happened to me that day, propped against the cock of hay, the sun shining, a breeze commencing, the clouds like cruisers in the heavens on their way to some distant port. I had closed my eyes, and then the cold thing hit the palm of my hand, fitting it exactly, and my fingers came over it to further the hold on it and to guess what it was. I did not dare say in case I should be wrong. It was, of course, a little bottle, with a screw-on cap and a label adhering to one side, but it was too much to hope that it would be my favorite perfume, the one called Mischief. She was urging me to guess. I feared that it might be an empty bottle, though such a gift would not be wholly unwelcome, since the remains of the smell always lingered; or that it might be a cheaper perfume, a less mysterious one named after a carnation or a poppy, a perfume that did not send shivers of joy down my throat and through my swallow to my very heart. At last I opened my eyes, and there it was, my most prized thing, in a little dark-blue bottle with a silverish label and a little rubber stopper, and inside, the precious stuff itself. I unscrewed the cap, lifted off the little rubber top, and a drop of the precious stuff was assigned to the flat of my finger and then conveyed to a particular spot in the hollow behind the left ear. She did exactly the same, and we kissed each other and breathed in the rapturous smell. The smell of hay intervened, so we ran to where there was no hay and kissed again. That moment had an air of mystery and sanctity about it, what with the surprise and our speechlessness, and a realization somewhere in the back of my mind that we were engaged in murky business indeed and that our larking days were over.

If things went well my mother had a saying that it was all too good to be true. It proved prophetic the following Saturday, because as my hair was being washed at the kitchen table, Eily arrived and sat at the end of the table and kept snapping her fingers in my direction. When I looked up from my expanse of suds, I saw that she was on the verge of tears and was blotchy all over. My mother almost scalded me, because in welcoming Eily she had forgotten to add the cold water to the pot of boiling water, and I screamed and leaped about the kitchen shouting hellfire and purgatory. Afterward Eily and I went around to the front of the house and sat on the step, where she told me that all was U.P. She had gone to him, as was her wont, under the bridge, where he did a spot of fishing each Friday, and he told her to make herself scarce. She refused, whereupon he moved downstream, and the moment she followed, he waded into the water. He kept telling her to beat it, beat it. She sat on the little milk stool, where he in fact had been sitting; then he did a terrible thing, which was to cast his rod in her direction and almost remove one of her eyes with the nasty hook. She burst into tears, and I began to plait her hair for comfort's sake. She swore that she would throw herself in the selfsame river before the night was out, then said it was only a lovers' quarrel, then said that he would have to see her, and finally announced that her heart was utterly broken, in smithereens. I had the little bottle of perfume in my pocket, and I held it up to the light to show how sparing I had been with it, but she was interested in nothing, only the ways and means of recovering him, or then again of taking her own life. Apart from drowning, she considered hanging, the intake of a bottle of Jeyes Fluid, or a few of the grains of strychnine that her father had for foxes.

Her father was a very gruff man who never spoke to the family except to order his meals and to tell the girls to mind their books. He himself had never gone to school, but had great acumen in the buying and selling of cattle and sheep, and put that down to the fact that he had met the scholars. He was an old man with an atrocious temper, and once on a fair day had ripped the clothing off an auctioneer who tried to diddle him over the price of an old Aladdin lamp.

My mother came to sit with us, and this alarmed me, since my mother never took the time to sit, either indoors or outdoors. She began to talk to Eily about knitting, about a new tweedex wool, asking if she secured some would Eily help her knit a three-quarter-length jacket. Eily had knitted lots of things for us, including the dress I was wearing—a salmon pink, with scalloped edges and a border of white angora decorating those edges. At that very second, as I had the angora to my face tickling it, my mother said to Eily that once she had gone to a fortune-teller, had removed her wedding ring as a decoy, and when the fortune-teller asked was she married, she had replied no, whereupon the fortune-teller said, "How come you have four children?" My mother said they were uncanny, those ladies, with their gypsy blood and their clairvoyant powers. I guessed exactly what Eily was thinking: Could we find a fortune-teller or a witch who could predict her future?

There was a witch twenty miles away who ran a public house and who was notorious, but who only took people on a whim. When my mother ran off to see if it was a fox because of the racket in the hen house, I said to Eily that

instead of consulting a witch we ought first to resort to
other things, such as novenas, putting wedding cake under
our pillows, or gathering bottles of dew in the early morning and putting them in a certain fort to make a wish.
Anyhow, how could we get to a village twenty miles away,
unless it was on foot or by bicycle, and neither of us had a
machine. Nevertheless, the following Sunday we were to
be found setting off with a bottle of tea, a little puncture
kit, and eight shillings, which was all the money we managed to scrape together.

We were not long started when Eily complained of feeling weak, and suddenly the bicycle was wobbling all over
the road, and she came a cropper as she tried to slow it
down by heading for a grass bank. Her brakes were nonex-
istent, as indeed were mine. They were borrowed bicycles.
I had to use the same method to dismount, and the two of
us with our front wheels wedged into the bank and our
handlebars askew, caused a passing motorist to call out
that we were a right pair of Mohawks and a danger to the
county council.

I gave her a sup of tea, and forced on her one of the eggs
which we had stolen from various nests and which were
intended as a bribe for our witch. Along with the eggs we
had a little flitch of home-cured bacon. She cracked it on
the handlebars and, with much persuasion from me, swal-
lowed it whole, saying it was worse than castor oil. It being
Sunday, she recalled other Sundays and where she would
be at that exact moment, and she prayed to St. Anthony to
please bring him back. We had heard that he went to Limerick most weekends now, and there was rumor that he was

going out with a bacon curer's daughter and that they were getting engaged.

The woman who opened the side door of the pub said that the witch did not live there any longer. She was very cross, had eyebrows that met, and these as well as the hairs in her head were a yellowish gray. She told us to leave her threshold at once, and how dare we intrude upon her Sunday leisure. She closed the door in our faces. I said to Eily, "That's her." And just as we were screwing up our courage to knock again, she reopened the door and said who in the name of Jacob had sent us. I said we'd come a long way, miles and miles; I showed the eggs and the bacon in its dusting of saltpeter, and she said she was extremely busy, seeing as it was her birthday and that sons and daughters and cousins were coming for a high tea. She opened and closed the door numerous times, and through it all we stood our ground, until finally we were brought in, but it was my fortune she wanted to tell. The kitchen was tiny and stuffy, and the same linoleum was on the floor as on the little wobbling table. There was a little wooden armchair for her, a long stool for visitors, and a stove that was smoking. Two rhubarb tarts were cooling on top, and that plus a card were the only indications of a birthday celebration. A small man, her husband, excused himself and wedged sideways through another door. I pleaded with her to take Eily rather than me, and after much dithering, and even going out to the garden to empty tea leaves, she said that maybe she would, but that we were pests, the pair of us. I was sent to join her husband in the little pantry, and was nearly smothered from the puffing of his pipe. There

was also a strong smell of flour, and no furniture except a
sewing machine with a half-finished garment, a shift,
wedged in under the needle. He talked in a whisper, said
that Mau Mau would come to Ireland and that St. Colum-
bus would rise from his grave, to make it once again the
island of saints and scholars. I was certain that I would
suffocate. Yet it was worth it. Eily was jubilant. Things
could not have been better. The witch had not only seen
his initial, J, but seen it twice in a concoction that she had
done with the whites of one of the eggs and some gruel.
Yes, things had been bad, very bad, there had been griev-
ous misunderstandings, but all was to be changed, and
leaning across the table, she said to Eily, "Ah sure, you'll
end your days with him."

Cycling home was a joy; we spun downhill, saying to hell
with safety, to hell with brakes, saluted strangers, admired
all the little cottages and the outhouses and the milk tanks
and the whining mongrels, and had no nerves passing the
haunted house. In fact, we would have liked to see an
apparition on that most buoyant of days. When we got to
the crossroads that led to our own village, Eily had a strong
presentiment, as indeed had I, that he would be there waiting for us, contrite, in a hair shirt, on bended knees. But he
was not. There was the usual crowd of lads playing pitch
and toss. A couple of the younger ones tried to impede us
by standing in front of the bikes, and Eily blushed red. She
was a favorite with everyone that summer, and she had a
different dress for every day of the week. She was called a
fashion plate. We said good night and knew that it did not
matter, that though he had not been waiting for us, before

long he and Eily would be united. She resolved to be
patient and be a little haughty and not seek him out.

Three weeks later, on a Saturday night, my mother was
soaking her feet in a mixture of warm water and washing
soda when a rap came on the scullery window. We both
trembled. There was a madman who had taken up resi-
dence in a bog hole and we were certain that it must be
him. "Call your father," she said. My father had gone to bed
in a huff, because she had given him a boiled egg instead
of a fry for his tea. I didn't want to leave her alone and
unattended, so I yelled up to my father, and at the same
time a second assault was delivered on the windowpane. I
heard the words "Sir, sir."

It was Eily's father, since he was the only person who
called my father sir. When we opened the door to him, the
first thing I saw was the slash hook in his hand, and then
the condition of his hair, which was upstanding and wild.
He said, "I'll hang, draw, and quarter him," and my mother
said, "Come in, Mr. Hogan," not knowing whom this
graphic fate was intended for. He said he had found his
daughter in the lime kiln, with the bank clerk, in the most
satanic position, with her belly showing.

My first thought was one of delight at their reunion, and
then I felt piqued that Eily hadn't told me but had chosen
instead to meet him at night in that disused kiln, which
reeked of damp. Better the woods, I thought, and the call
of the cuckoo, and myself keeping some kind of watch,
though invariably glued to the bark of a tree.

He said he had come to fetch a lantern, to follow them
as they had scattered in different directions, and he did not

know which of them to kill first. My father, whose good humor was restored by this sudden and unexpected intrusion, said to hold on for a moment, to step inside so that they could consider a plan of campaign. Mr. Hogan left his cap on the step, a thing he always did, and my mother begged him to bring it in, since the new pup ate every article of clothing that it could find. Only that very morning my mother looked out on the field and thought it was flakes of snow, but in fact it was her line of washing, chewed to pieces. He refused to bring in his cap, which to me was a perfect example of how stubborn he was and how awkward things were going to be. At once, my father ordered my mother to make tea, and though still gruff, there was between them now an understanding, because of the worse tragedy that loomed. My mother seemed the most perturbed, made a hopeless cup of tea, cut the bread in agricultural hunks, and did everything wrong, as if she herself had just been found out in some base transaction. After the men had gone out on their search party, she got me to go down on my knees to pray with her; I found it hard to pray, because I was already thinking of the flogging I would get for being implicated. She cross-examined me. Did I know anything about it? Had Eily ever met him? Why had she made herself so much style, especially that slit skirt.

I said no to everything. These no's were much too hastily delivered, and if my mother had not been so busy cogitating and surmising, she would have suspected something for sure. Kneeling there, I saw them trace every movement of ours, get bits of information from this one and that one, the so-called cousins, the woman who had promised us the gooseberries, and Mrs. Bolan. I knew we had no hope. Eily! Her most precious thing was gone, her jewel. The inside of one was like a little watch, and once the jewel or jewels were gone, the outside was nothing but a sham. I saw her die in the cold lime kiln and then again in a sick room, and then stretched out on an operating table, the very way I used to be. She had joined that small sodality of scandalous women who had conceived children without securing fathers and who were damned in body and soul. Had they convened they would have been a band of seven or eight, and might have sent up an unholy wail to their Maker and their covert seducers. The one thing I could not endure was the thought of her stomach protuberant and a baby coming out saying "Ba ba." Had I had the chance to see her, I should have suggested that we run away with gypsies.

Poor Eily, from then on she was kept under lock and key, and allowed out only to Mass, and then so concealed was she, with a mantilla over her face, that she was not even able to make a lip sign to me. Never did she look so beautiful as those subsequent Sundays in chapel, her hair and her face veiled, her pensive eyes peering through. I once sat directly in front of her, and when we stood up for the first Gospel, I stared up into her face and got such a dig in the ribs from my mother that I toppled over.

A mission commenced the following week, and a strange priest with a beautiful accent and a strong sense of rhetoric delivered the sermons each evening. It was better than a theater—the chapel in a state of hush, ladders of candles, all lit, extra flowers on the altar, a medley of smells, the white linen, and the place so packed that we youngsters had to sit on the altar steps and saw everything clearer, including the priest's Adam's apple as it bobbed up and down. Always I could sight Eily, hemmed in by her mother and some other old woman, pale and impassive, and I was certain that she was about to die. On the evening that the sermon centered on the sixth commandment, we youngsters were kept outside until Benediction time. We spent the time wandering through the stalls, looking at the tiers of rosary beads that were as dazzling as necklaces, all hanging side by side and quivering in the breeze, all colors, and of different stones, then of course the bright scapulars, and all kinds of little medals and beautiful crucifixes that were bigger than the girth of one's hand, and even some that had a little cavity within, where a relic was contained, and also beautiful prayer books and missals, some with gold edging, and little holdalls made of filigree.

When we trooped in for the Benediction, Eily slipped me a holy picture. It had Christ on the cross and a verse beneath it: "You have but one soul to save/One God to love and serve/One eternity to prepare for/Death will come soon./Judgment will follow—and then/Heaven or Hell forever." I was musing on it and swallowing back my tears at the very moment that Eily began to retch and was hefted out by four of the men. They bore her aloft as if she were a corpse on a litter. I said to my mother that most likely Eily would die, and my mother said if only such a solution could occur. My mother already knew. The next evening Eily was in our house, in the front room, and though I was not admitted, I listened at the door and ran off only when there was a scream or a blow or a thud. She was being questioned about each and every event, and about the bank clerk and what exactly were her associations with him. She said no, over and over again, and at moments was quite defiant and, as they said, an "upstart." One minute they were asking her kindly, another minute they were heckling, another minute her father swore that it was to the lunatic asylum that she would be sent, and then at once her mother was condemning her for not having milked for two weeks.

They were inconsistency itself. How could she have milked since she was locked in the room off the kitchen, where they stowed the oats and which was teeming with mice. I knew for a fact that her meals—a hunk of bread and a mug of weak tea—were handed into her twice a day, and that she had nothing else to do, only cry and think and sit herself upon the oats and run her fingers through it, and probably have to keep making noises to frighten off the mice. When they were examining her, my mother was the most reasonable, but also the most exacting. My mother would ask such things as "Where did you meet? How long were you together? Were others present?" Eily denied ever having met him and was spry enough to say, "What do you take me for, Mrs. Brady, a hussy?" But that incurred some sort of a belt from her father, because I heard my mother say that there was no need to resort to savagery. I almost swooned when on the glass panel of our hall door I saw a shadow, then knuckles, and through the glass the appearance of a brown habit, such as the missioner wore.

He saw Eily alone; we all waited in the kitchen, the men supping tea, my mother segmenting a grapefruit to offer to the priest. It seemed odd fare to give him in the evening, but she was used to entertaining priests only at breakfast time, when one came every five or ten years to say Mass in the house to rebless it and put paid to the handiwork of the devil. When he was leaving, the missioner shook hands with each of us, then patted my hair. Watching his sallow face and his rimless spectacles, and drinking in his beautiful speaking voice, I thought that if I were Eily I would prefer him to the bank clerk, and would do anything to be in his company.

I had one second with Eily, while they all trooped out to open the gate for the priest and to wave him off. She said for God's sake not to spill on her. Then she was taken upstairs by my mother, and when they reemerged, Eily was wearing one of my mother's mackintoshes, a Mrs. Miniver hat, and a pair of old sunglasses. It was a form of disguise, since they were setting out on a journey. Eily's father wanted to put a halter around her, but my mother said it wasn't the Middle Ages. I was enjoined to wash cups and saucers, to empty the ashtray, and to plump the cushions again, but once they were gone, I was unable to move because of a dreadful pain that gripped the lower part of my back and stomach. I was convinced that I, too, was having a baby and that if I were to move or part my legs, some freakish thing would come tumbling out.

The following morning Eily's father went to the bank, where he broke two glass panels, sent coins flying about the place, assaulted the bank manager, and tried to saw off part of the bank clerk's anatomy. The two customers—the butcher and the undertaker—had to intervene, and the lady clerk, who was in the cloakroom, managed to get to the telephone to call the barracks. When the sergeant came

on the scene, Eily's father was being held down, his hands
tied with a skipping rope, but he was still trying to aim a
kick at the blackguard who had ruined his daughter. Very
quickly the sergeant got the gist of things. It was agreed
that Jack—that was the culprit's name—would come to
their house that evening. Though the whole occasion was
to be fraught with misfortune, my mother, upon hearing
of it, said some sort of buffet would have to be considered.

It proved to be an arduous day. The oats had to be shov-
eled out of the room, and the women were left to do it,
since my father was busy seeing the solicitor and the priest,
and Eily's father remained in the town, boasting about
what he would have done to the bugger if only the sergeant
hadn't come on the scene.

Eily was silence itself. She didn't even smile at me when
I brought the basket of groceries that her mother had sent
to fetch. Her mother kept referring to the fact that they
would never provide bricks and mortar for the new house
now. For years she and her husband had been skimping and
saving, intending to build a house two fields nearer the
road. It was to be identical to their own house, that is to
say, a cement two-story house, but with the addition of a
lavatory and a tiny hall inside the front door, so that, as she
said, if company came, they could be vetted there instead
of plunging straight into the kitchen. She was a backward
woman, and probably because of living in the fields she had
no friends and had never stepped inside anyone else's door.
She always washed outdoors at the rain barrel, and never
called her husband anything but mister. Unpacking the
groceries, she said that it was a pity to waste them on him,
and the only indulgence she permitted herself was to smell

the things, especially the packet of raspberry and custard biscuits. There was blackcurrant jam, a Scribona Swiss roll, a tin of herring in tomato sauce, a loaf, and a large tin of fruit cocktail.

Eily kept whitening and rewhitening her buckskin shoes. No sooner were they out on the window than she would bring them in and whiten again. The women were in the room putting the oats into sacks. They didn't have much to say. My mother always used to laugh, because when they met, Mrs. Hogan used to say, "Any newses?" and look up at her with that wild stare, opening her mouth to show the big gaps between her front teeth, but the "newses" had at last come to her own door, and though she must have minded dreadfully, she seemed vexed more than ashamed, as if it was inconvenience rather than disgrace that had hit her. But from that day on, she almost stopped calling Eily by her pet name, which was Alannah.

I said to Eily that if she liked we could make toffee, because making toffee always humored her. She pretended not to hear. Even to her mother she refused to speak, and when asked a question she bared her teeth like one of the dogs. She wanted one of the dogs, Spot, to bite me, and led him to me by the ear, but he was more interested in a sheep's head that I had brought from the town. It was an arduous day, what with carting out the oats in cans and buckets, and refilling it into sacks, moving a table in there and tea chests, finding suitable covers for them, laying the table properly, getting rid of all the cobwebs in the corners, sweeping up the soot that had fallen down the chimney, and even running up a little curtain. Eily had to hem it, and as she sat outside the back door, I could see her face and her expression; she looked very stubborn and not nearly so amenable as before. My mother provided a roast chicken, some pickles, and freshly boiled beets. She skinned the hot beets with her hands and said, "Ah, you've made your bed now," but Eily gave no evidence of having heard. She simply washed her face in the aluminum basin, combed her hair severely back, put on her whitened shoes, and then turned around to make sure that the seams of her stockings were straight. Her father came home drunk, and he looked like a younger man, trotting up the fields in his oatmeal-colored socks—he'd lost his shoes. When he saw the sitting room that had up to then been the oats room, he exclaimed, took off his hat to it, and said, "Am I in my own house at all, mister?" My father arrived full of important news which, as he kept saying, he would discuss later. We waited in a ring, seated around the fire, and the odd words said were said only by the men, and then without any point. They discussed a beast that had had some ailment.

The dogs were the first to let us know. We all jumped up and looked through the window. The bank clerk was coming on foot, and my mother said to look at that swagger, and wasn't it the swagger of a hobo. Eily ran to look in the mirror that was fixed to the window ledge. For some extraordinary reason my father went out to meet him and straightaway produced a pack of cigarettes. The two of them came in smoking, and he was shown to the sitting room, which was directly inside the door to the left. There were no drinks on offer, since the women decided that the men might only get obstreperous. Eily's father kept pointing to the glories of the room, and lifted up a bit of cretonne, to make sure that it was a tea chest underneath and not a piece of pricy mahogany. My father said, "Well, Mr. Jacksie, you'll have to do your duty by her and make an honest woman of her." Eily was standing by the window, looking out at the oncoming dark. The bank clerk said, "Why so?" and whistled in a way that I had heard him whistle in the past. He did not seem put out. I was afraid that on impulse he might rush over and put his hands somewhere on Eily's person. Eily's father mortified us all by saying she had a porker in her, and the bank clerk said so had many a lass, whereupon he got a slap across the face and was told to sit down and behave himself.

From that moment on, he must have realized he was lost. On all other occasions I had seen him wear a khaki jacket and plus fours, but that evening he wore a brown suit that gave him a certain air of reliability and dullness. He didn't say a word to Eily, or even look in her direction, as she sat on a little stool staring out the window and biting on the little lavaliere that she wore around her neck. My father said he had been pup enough and the only thing to do was to own up to it and marry her. The bank clerk put forward three objections—one, that he had no house; two, that he had no money; and three, that he was not considering marrying. During the supper Eily's mother refused to sit down and stayed in the kitchen, nursing the big tin of fruit cocktail and having feeble jabs at it with the old iron tin opener. She talked aloud to herself about the folks "hither" in the room and what a sorry pass things had come to. As usual, my mother ate only the pope's nose, and served the men the breasts of chicken. Matters changed every other second, they were polite to him, remembering his status as a bank clerk, then they were asking him what kind of crops grew in his part of the country, and then again they would refer to him as if he were not there, saying, "The pup likes his bit of meat." He was told that he would marry her on the Wednesday week, that he was being transferred from the bank, that he would go with his new wife and take rooms in a midland town. He just shrugged, and I was thinking that he would probably vanish on the morrow, but I didn't know that they had alerted everyone and that when he did in fact try to leave at dawn the following morning, three strong men impeded him and brought him up the mountain for a drive in their lorry. For a week after, he was indisposed, and it is said that his black eyes were bulbous. It left a permanent hole in his lower cheek, as if a little pebble of flesh had been tweezed out of him.

Anyhow, they discussed the practicalities of the wedding while they ate their fruit cocktail. It was served in the little carnival dishes, and I thought of the numerous operations that Nuala had done, and how if it was left to Eily and me, things would not be nearly so crucial. I did not want her to have to marry him, and I almost blurted that out. But the plans were going ahead; he was being told that it would cost him ten pounds, that it would be in the sacristy of the Catholic church, since he was a Protestant, and there were to be no guests except those present and Eily's former teacher, a Miss Melody. Even her sister, Nuala, was not going to be told until after the event. They kept asking him was that clear, and he kept saying, "Oh yeah," as if it were a simple matter of whether he would have more fruit cocktail or not. The number of cherries were few and far between, and for some reason had a faint mauve hue to them. I got one and my mother passed me hers. Eily ate well but listlessly, as if she weren't there at all. Toward the end my father sang "Master McGrath," a song about a greyhound, and Mr. Hogan told the ghost story about seeing the headless liveried man at a crossroads when he was a boy.

Going down the field, Eily was told to walk on ahead with her intended, probably so that she could discuss her trousseau or any last-minute things. The stars were bewitching, and the moonlight cast as white a glow as if it were morning and the world was veiled with frost. Eily and he walked in utter silence. At last, she looked up at him and said something, and all he did was to draw away from her; there was such a distance between them that a cart or a car could pass through. She edged a little to the right to get nearer, and as she did, he moved farther away, so that eventually she was on the edge of a path and he was right by the hedge, hitting the bushes with a bit of a stick he had picked up. We followed behind, the grownups discussing whether or not it would rain the next day while I wondered what Eily had tried to say to him.

They met twice more before the wedding, once in the sitting room of the hotel, when the traveling solicitor drew up the papers guaranteeing her a dowry of two hundred pounds, and once in the city, when he was sent with her to the jeweler's to buy a wedding ring. It was the same city as where he had been seeing the bacon curer's daughter, and Eily said that in the jeweler's he expressed the wish that she would drop dead. At the wedding breakfast itself there were only sighs and tears, and the teacher, as was her wont, stood in front of the fire and, mindless of the mixed company, hitched up her dress behind, the better to warm the cheeks of her bottom. In his giving-away speech, my father said they had only to make the best of it. Eily sniveled, her mother wept and wept and said, "Oh, Alannah, Alannah," while the groom muttered, "Once bitten, twice shy." The reception was in their new lodgings, and my mother said that she thought it was bad form the way the landlady included herself in the proceedings. My mother also said that their household utensils were pathetic, two forks, two knives, two spoons, an old kettle, an egg saucepan, a primus, and, as she said, not even a nice enamel bin for the bread but a rusted biscuit tin. When they came to leave, Eily tried to dart into the back of the car, tried it more than once, just like an animal trying to get back to its lair.

On returning home my mother let me put on her lipstick and praised me untowardly for being such a good, such a pure little girl, and never did I feel so guilty, because of the leading part I had played in Eily's romance. The only thing that my mother had eaten at the wedding was a jelly made with milk. We tried it the following Sunday, a raspberry-flavored jelly made with equal quantities of milk and water—and then whisked. It was like a beautiful pink tongue, dotted with spittle, and it tasted slippery. I had not been found out, had received no punishment, and life was getting back to normal again. I gargled with salt and water, on Sundays longed for visitors that never came, and on Monday mornings had all my books newly covered so that the teacher would praise me. Ever since the scandal she was enjoining us to go home in pairs, to speak Irish, and not to walk with any sense of provocation.

Yet she herself stood by the fire grate and, after having hitched up her dress, petted herself. When she lost her temper, she threw chalk or implements at us, and used very bad language.

It was a wonderful year for lilac, and the windowsills used to be full of it, first the big moist bunches, with the lovely cool green leaves, and then a wilting display, and following that, the seeds in pools all over the sill and the purple itself much sadder and more dolorous than when first plucked off the trees.

When I daydreamed, which was often, it hinged on Eily. Did she have a friend, did her husband love her, was she homesick, and above all, was her body swelling up? She wrote to her mother every second week. Her mother used to come with her apron on, and the letter in one of those pockets, and sit on the back step and hesitate before reading it. She never came in, being too shy, but she would sit there while my father fetched her a cup of raspberry cordial. We all had sweet tooths. The letters told next to nothing, only such things as that their chimney had caught fire, or a boy herding goats found an old coin in a field, or could her mother root out some old clothes from a trunk and send them to her as she hadn't got a stitch. " 'Tis style enough she has," her mother would say bitterly, and then advise that it was better to cut my hair and not have me go around in ringlets, because, as she said, "Fine feathers make fine birds." Now and then she would cry and then feed the birds the crumbs of the biscuit or shortbread that my mother had given her.

She liked the birds and in secret in her own yard made little perches for them, and if you please hung bits of colored rags and the shaving mirror for them to amuse themselves by. My mother had made a quilt for Eily, and I believe that was the only wedding present she received. They parceled it together. It was a red flannel quilt, lined with white, and had a herringbone stitch around the edge. It was not like the big soft quilt that once occupied the entire window of the draper's, a pink satin on which one's body could bask, then levitate. One day her mother looked right at me and said, "Has she passed any more worms?" I had passed a big tapeworm, and that was a talking point for a week or so after the furor of the wedding had died down. Then she gave me half a crown. It was some way of thanking me for being a friend of Eily's. When her son was born, the family received a wire. He was given the name of Jack, the same as his father, and I thought how the witch had been right when she had seen the initial twice, but how we had misconstrued it and took it to be glad tidings.

Eily began to grow odd, began talking to herself, and then her lovely hair began to fall out in clumps. I would hear her mother tell my mother these things. The news came in snatches, first from a family who had gone up there to rent grazing, and then from a private nurse who had to give Eily pills and potions. Eily's own letters were disconnected and she asked about dead people or people she'd hardly known. Her mother meant to go by bus one day and stay overnight, but she postponed it until her arthritis got too bad and she was not able to go out at all.

Four years later, at Christmastime, Eily, her husband, and their three children paid a visit home, and she kept eyeing everything and asking people to please stop staring at her, and then she went around the house and looked under the beds, for some male spy whom she believed to be there. She was dressed in brown and had brown fur-backed gloves. Her husband was very suave, had let his hair grow long, and during the tea kept pressing his knee against mine and asking me which did I like best, sweet or savory. The only moment of levity was when the three children, clothes and all, got into a pig trough and began to splash in it. Eily laughed her head off as they were being hosed down by her mother. Then they had to be put into the settle bed, alongside the sacks of flour and the brooms and the bric-à-brac, while their clothes were first washed and then put on a little wooden horse to dry before the fire. They were laughing, but their teeth chattered. Eily didn't remember me very clearly and kept asking me if I was the oldest or the middle girl in the family. We heard later that her husband got promoted and was running a little shop and had young girls working as his assistants.

I was pregnant, and walking up a street in a city with my own mother, under not very happy circumstances, when we saw this wild creature coming toward us, talking and debating to herself. Her hair was gray and frizzed, her costume was streelish, and she looked at us, and then peered, as if she was going to pounce on us; then she started to laugh at us, or rather, to sneer, and she stalked away and pounced on some other persons. My mother said, "I think that was Eily," and warned me not to look back. We both walked on, in terror, and then ducked into the porchway of a shop, so that we could follow her with our eyes without ourselves being seen. She was being avoided by all sorts of people, and by now she was shouting something and brandishing her fist and struggling to get heard. I shook, as indeed the child within me was induced to shake, and for one moment I wanted to go down that street to her, but my mother held me back and said that she was dangerous, and that in my condition I must not go. I did not need much in the way of persuading. She moved on; by now several people were laughing and looking after her, and I was unable to move, and all the gladness of our summer day, and a little bottle of Mischief pressed itself into the palm of my hand again, and I saw her lithe and beautiful as she once was, and in the street a great flood of light pillared itself around a little cock of hay while the two of us danced with joy.

I did go in search of her years later. My husband waited up at the cross and I went down the narrow steep road with my son, who was thrilled to be approaching a shop. Eily was behind the counter, her head bent over a pile of bills that she was attaching to a skewer. She looked up and smiled. The same face but much coarser. Her hair was permed and a newly pared pencil protruded from it. She was pleased to see me, and at once reached out and handed my son a fistful of rainbow toffees.

It was the very same as if we'd parted only a little while ago. She didn't shake hands or make any special fuss, she simply said, "Talk of an angel," because she had been thinking of me that very morning. Her children were helping; one was weighing sugar, the little girl was funneling castor oil into four-ounce bottles, and her oldest son was up on a ladder fixing a flex to a ceiling light. He said my name, said it with a sauciness as soon as she introduced me, but she told him to whist. For her own children she had no time, because they were already grown, but for my son he was full of welcome and kept saying he was a cute little fellow. She weighed him on the big meal scales and then let him scoop the grain with a little trowel, and let it slide down the length of his arm and made him gurgle.

People kept coming in and out, and she went on talking to me while serving them. She was complete mistress of her surroundings and said what a pity that her husband was away, off on the lorry, doing the door-to-door orders. He had given up banking, found the business more profitable. She winked each time she hit the cash register, letting me see what an expert she was. Whenever there was a lull, I thought of saying something, but my son's pranks commandeered the occasion. She was very keen to offer me something and ripped the glass paper off a two-pound box of chocolates and laid them before me, slantwise, propped against a can or something. They were eminently inviting, and when I refused, she made some reference to the figure.

"You were always too generous," I said, sounding like my mother or some stiff relation.

"Go on," she said, and biffed me.

It seemed the right moment to broach it, but how?

"How are you?" I said. She said that, as I could see, she was topping, getting on a bit, and the children were great sorts, and the next time I came I'd have to give her notice so that we could have a singsong. I didn't say that my husband was up at the road and by now would be looking at his watch and saying "Damn" and maybe would have got out to polish or do some cosseting to the vintage motorcar that he loved so. I said, and again it was lamentable, "Remember the old days, Eily."

"Not much," she said.

"The good old days," I said.

"They're all much of a muchness," she said.

"Bad," I said.

"No, busy," she said. My first thought was that they must have drugged the feelings out of her, they must have given her strange brews, and along with quelling her madness, they had taken her spark away. To revive a dead friendship is almost always a risk, and we both knew it but tried to be polite.

She kissed me and put a little holy water on my forehead, delving it in deeply, as if I were dough. They waved to us, and my son could not return those waves, encumbered as he was with the various presents that both the children and Eily had showered on him. It was beginning to spot with rain, and what with that and the holy water and the red rowan tree bright and instinct with life, I thought that ours indeed was a land of shame, a land of murder, and a land of strange, throttled, sacrificial women.

The Aran Islands

J. M. Synge

I AM IN ARANMOR, sitting over a turf fire, listening to a murmur of Gaelic that is rising from a little public house under my room.

The steamer which comes to Aran sails according to the tide, and it was six o'clock this morning when we left the quay of Galway in a dense shroud of mist.

A low lime of shore was visible at first on the right between the movement of the waves and fog, but when we

JOHN MILLINGTON SYNGE (1871–1909) was born in Rathfarnham, Dublin. Synge was an important figure in the Irish Literary Revival and was one of the founders of the Abbey Theatre. He is perhaps best known for his drama *The Playboy of the Western World*, which caused riots in Dublin during its opening run at the Abbey Theatre. While living in Paris he met William Butler Yeats who persuaded him to visit the Aran Islands. All of Synge's plays reflect his experiences living on the Aran Islands. His journal *The Aran Islands* was completed in 1901 and published in 1907 with illustrations by Jack Yeats. Synge suffered from Hodgkin's disease, a form of cancer that was untreatable at the time. He died just a few weeks short of his thirty-eighth birthday.

came further it was lost sight of, and nothing could be seen but the mist curling in the rigging, and a small circle of foam.

There were few passengers; a couple of men going out with young pigs tied loosely in sacking, three or four young girls who sat in the cabin with their heads completely twisted in their shawls, and a builder, on his way to repair the pier at Kilronan, who walked up and down and talked with me.

In about three hours Aran came in sight. A dreary rock appeared at first sloping up from the sea into the fog; then, as we drew nearer, a coastguard station and the village.

A little later I was wandering out along the one good roadway of the island, looking over low walls on either side into small flat fields of naked rock. I have seen nothing so desolate. Grey floods of water were sweeping everywhere upon the limestone, making at times a wild torrent of the road, which twined continually over low hills and cavities in the rock or passed between a few small fields of potatoes or grass hidden away in corners that had shelter. Whenever the cloud lifted I could see the edge of the sea below me on the right, and the naked ridge of the island above me on the other side. Occasionally I passed a lonely chapel or schoolhouse, or a line of stone pillars with crosses above them and inscriptions asking a prayer for the soul of the person they commemorated.

I met few people; but here and there a band of tall girls passed me on their way to Kilronan, and called out to me with humorous wonder, speaking English with a slight foreign intonation that differed a good deal from the brogue of Galway. The rain and cold seemed to have no influence on their vitality, and as they hurried past me with eager laughter and great talking in Gaelic, they left the wet masses of rock more desolate than before.

A little after midday when I was coming back one old half-blind man spoke to me in Gaelic, but, in general, I was surprised at the abundance and fluency of the foreign tongue.

In the afternoon the rain continued, so I sat here in the inn looking out through the mist at a few men who were unlading hookers that had come in with turf from Connemara, and at the long-legged pigs that were playing in the surf. As the fishermen came in and out of the public house underneath my room, I could hear through the broken panes that a number of them still used Gaelic, though it seems to be falling out of use among the younger people of this village.

The old woman of the house had promised to get me a teacher of the language, and after a while I heard a shuffling on the stairs, and the old dark man I had spoken to in the morning groped his way into the room.

I brought him over to the fire, and we talked for many hours. He told me that he had known Petrie and Sir William Wilde, and many living antiquarians, and had taught Irish to Dr Finck and Dr Pedersen, and given stories to Mr. Curtin of America. A little after middle age he had fallen over a cliff, and since then he had had little eyesight, and a trembling of his hands and head.

As we talked he sat huddled together over the fire, shaking and blind, yet his face was indescribably pliant, lighting up with an ecstasy of humor when he told me anything that had a point of wit or malice, and growing sombre and desolate again when he spoke of religion or the fairies.

He had great confidence in his own powers and talent, and in the superiority of his stories over all other stories in the world. When we were speaking of Mr. Curtin, he told me that this gentleman had brought out a volume of his Aran stories in America, and made five hundred pounds by the sale of them.

"And what do you think he did then?" he continued; "he wrote a book of his own stories after making that lot of money with mine. And he brought them out, and the divil a halfpenny did he get for them. Would you believe that?"

Afterwards he told me how one of his children had been taken by the fairies.

One day a neighbor was passing, and she said, when she saw it on the road, "That's a fine child."

Its mother tried to say, "God bless it," but something choked the words in her throat.

A while later they found a wound on its neck, and for three nights the house was filled with noises.

"I never wear a shirt at night," he said, "but I got up out of my bed, all naked as I was, when I heard the noises in the house, and lighted a light, but there was nothing in it."

Then a dummy came and made signs of hammering nails in a coffin.

The next day the seed potatoes were full of blood, and the child told his mother that he was going to America.

That night it died, and "believe me," said the old man, "the fairies were in it."

When he went away, a little bare-footed girl was sent up

with turf and the bellows to make a fire that would last for the evening.

She was shy, yet eager to talk, and told me that she had good spoken Irish, and was learning to read it in the school, and that she had been twice to Galway, though there are many grown women in the place who have never set a foot upon the mainland.

The rain has cleared off, and I have had my first real introduction to the island and its people.

I went out through Killeany—the poorest village in Aranmor—to a long neck of sandhill that runs out into the sea towards the southwest. As I lay there on the grass the clouds lifted from the Connemara mountains and, for a moment, the green undulating foreground, backed in the distance by a mass of hills, reminded me of the country near Rome. Then the dun topsail of a hooker swept above the edge of the sandhill and revealed the presence of the sea.

As I moved on a boy and a man came down from the next village to talk to me, and I found that here, at least, English was imperfectly understood. When I asked them if there were any trees in the island they held a hurried consultation in Gaelic, and then the man asked if "tree" meant the same thing as "bush," for if so there were a few in sheltered hollows to the east.

They walked on with me to the sound which separates this island from Inishmaan—the middle island of the group—and showed me the roll from the Atlantic running up between two walls of cliff.

They told me that several men had stayed on Inishmaan

to learn Irish, and the boy pointed out a line of hovels where they had lodged running like a belt of straw round the middle of the island. The place looked hardly fit for habitation. There was no green to be seen, and no sign of the people except these beehive-like roofs, and the outline of a Dun that stood out above them against the edge of the sky.

After a while my companions went away and two other boys came and walked at my heels, till I turned and made them talk to me. They spoke at first of their poverty, and then one of them said—

"I daresay you do have to pay ten shillings a week in the hotel?"

"More," I answered.

"Twelve?"

"More."

"Fifteen?"

"More still."

Then he drew back and did not question me any further, either thinking that I had lied to check his curiosity, or too awed by my riches to continue.

Repassing Killeany I was joined by a man who had spent twenty years in America, where he had lost his health and then returned, so long ago that he had forgotten English and could hardly make me understand him. He seemed hopeless, dirty, and asthmatic, and after going with me for a few hundred yards he stopped and asked for coppers. I had none left, so I gave him fill of tobacco, and he went back to his hovel.

When he was gone, two little girls took their place behind me and I drew them in turn into conversation.

They spoke with a delicate exotic intonation that was

full of charm, and told me with a sort of chant how they guide "ladies and gintlemins" in the summer to all that is worth seeing in their neighborhood, and sell them pampooties and maidenhair ferns, which are common among the rocks.

We were now in Kilronan, and as we parted they showed me holes in their own pampooties, or cowskin sandals, and asked me the price of new ones. I told them that my purse was empty, and then with a few quaint words of blessing they turned away from me and went down to the pier.

All this walk back had been extraordinarily fine. The intense insular clearness one sees only in Ireland, and after rain, was throwing out every ripple in the sea and sky, and every crevice in the hills beyond the bay.

This evening an old man came to see me, and said he had known a relative of mine who passed some time on this island forty-three years ago.

"I was standing under the pier-wall mending nets," he said, "when you came off the steamer, and I said to myself in that moment, if there is a man of the name of Synge left walking the world, it is that man yonder will be he."

He went on to complain in curiously simple yet dignified language of the changes that have taken place here since he left the island to go to sea before the end of his childhood.

"I have come back," he said, "to live in a bit of a house with my sister. The island is not the same at all to what it was. It is little good I can get from the people who are in it now, and anything I have to give them they don't care to have."

From what I hear this man seems to have shut himself up in a world of individual conceits and theories, and to live aloof at his trade of net-mending, regarded by the other islanders with respect and half-ironical sympathy.

A little later when I went down to the kitchen I found two men from Inishmaan who had been benighted on the island. They seemed a simpler and perhaps a more interesting type than the people here, and talked with careful English about the history of the Duns, and the Book of Ballymote, and the Book of Kells, and other ancient manuscripts, with the names of which they seemed familiar.

In spite of the charm of my teacher, the old blind man I met the day of my arrival, I have decided to move on to Inishmaan, where Gaelic is more generally used, and the life is perhaps the most primitive that is left in Europe.

I spent all this last day with my blind guide, looking at the antiquities that abound in the west or northwest of the island.

As we set out I noticed among the groups of girls who smiled at our fellowship—old Máirtín says we are like the cuckoo with its pipit—a beautiful oval face with the singularly spiritual expression that is so marked in one type of the West Ireland women. Later in the day, as the old man talked continually of the fairies and the women they have taken, it seemed that there was a possible link between the wild mythology that is accepted on the islands and the strange beauty of the women.

At midday we rested near the ruins of a house, and two beautiful boys came up and sat near us. Old Máirtín asked them why the house was in ruins, and who had lived in it.

"A rich farmer built it a while since," they said, "but after two years he was driven away by the fairy host."

The boys came on with us some distance to the north to visit one of the ancient beehive dwellings that is still in perfect preservation. When we crawled in on our hands and knees, and stood up in the gloom of the interior, old Máirtín took a freak of earthly humor and began telling what he would have done if he could have come in there when he was a young man and a young girl along with him.

Then he sat down in the middle of the floor and began to recite old Irish poetry, with an exquisite purity of intonation that brought tears to my eyes though I understood but little of the meaning.

On our way home he gave me the Catholic theory of the fairies.

When Lucifer saw himself in the glass he thought himself equal with God. Then the Lord threw him out of Heaven, and all the angels that belonged to him. While He was "chucking them out," an archangel asked Him to spare some of them, and those that were falling are in the air still, and have power to wreck ships, and to work evil in the world.

From this he wandered off into tedious matters of theology, and repeated many long prayers and sermons in Irish that he had heard from the priests.

A little further on we came to a slated house, and I asked him who was living in it.

"A kind of a schoolmistress," he said; then his old face puckered with a gleam of pagan malice.

"Ah, master," he said, "wouldn't it be fine to be in there, and to be kissing her?"

A couple of miles from this village we turned aside to look at an old ruined church of the Ceathrar Álainn (The Four Beautiful Persons), and a holy well near it that is famous for cures of blindness and epilepsy.

As we sat near the well a very old man came up from a cottage near the road, and told me how it had become famous.

"A woman of Sligo had a son who was born blind, and one night she dreamed that she saw an island with a blessed well in it that could cure her son. She told her dream in the morning, and an old man said it was of Aran she was after dreaming.

"She brought her son down by the coast of Galway, and came out in a curagh, and landed below where you see a bit of a cove.

"She walked up then to the house of my father—God rest his soul—and she told them what she was looking for.

"My father said that there was a well like what she had dreamed of, and that he would send a boy along with her to show her the way.

"There's no need, at all," said she; "haven't I seen it all in my dream?"

"Then she went out with the child and walked up to this well, and she kneeled down and began saying her prayers. Then she put her hand out for the water, and put it on his eyes, and the moment it touched him he called out: 'O mother, look at the pretty flowers!'"

After that Máirtín described the feats of poteen drinking and fighting that he did in his youth, and went on to talk of Diarmaid, who was the strongest man after Samson, and of one of the beds of Diarmaid and Gráinne, which is on the east of the island. He says that Diarmaid was killed by the druids, who put a burning shirt on him—a fragment of mythology that may connect Diarmaid with the legend of Hercules, if it is not due to the "learning" in some hedge-school master's ballad.

Then we talked about Inishmaan.

"You'll have an old man to talk with you over there," he said, "and tell you stories of the fairies, but he's walking about with two sticks under him this ten year. Did ever you hear what it is goes on four legs when it is young, and on two legs after that, and on three legs when it does be old?"

I gave him the answer.

"Ah, master," he said, "you're a cute one, and the blessing of God be on you. Well, I'm on three legs this minute, but the old man beyond is back on four; I don't know if I'm better than the way he is; he's got his sight and I'm only an old dark man."

I am settled at last on Inishmaan in a small cottage with a continual drone of Gaelic coming from the kitchen that opens into my room.

Early this morning the man of the house came over for me with a four-oared curagh—that is, a curagh with four rowers and four oars on either side, as each man uses two—and we set off a little before noon.

It gave me a moment of exquisite satisfaction to find myself moving away from civilization in this rude canvas canoe of a model that has served primitive races since men first went on the sea.

We had to stop for a moment at a hulk that is anchored in the bay, to make some arrangements for the fish-curing of the middle island, and my crew called out as soon as we were within earshot that they had a man with them who had been in France a month from this day.

When we started again, a small sail was run up in the bow, and we set off across the sound with a leaping oscillation that had no resemblance to the heavy movement of a boat.

The sail is only used as an aid, so the men continued to row after it had gone up, and as they occupied the four cross-seats I lay on the canvas at the stern and the frame of slender laths, which bent and quivered as the waves passed under them.

When we set off it was a brilliant morning of April, and the green, glittering waves seemed to toss the canoe among themselves, yet as we drew nearer this island a sudden thunderstorm broke out behind the rocks we were approaching, and lent a momentary tumult to this still vein of the Atlantic.

We landed at a small pier, from which a rude track leads up to the village between small fields and bare sheets of rock like those in Aranmor. The youngest son of my boatman, a boy of about seventeen, who is to be my teacher and guide, was waiting for me at the pier and guided me to his house, while the men settled the curagh and followed slowly with my baggage.

My room is at one end of the cottage, with a boarded floor and ceiling, and two windows opposite each other. Then there is the kitchen with earth floor and open rafters, and two doors opposite each other opening into the open air, but no windows. Beyond it there are two small rooms of half the width of the kitchen with one window apiece.

The kitchen itself, where I will spend most of my time, is full of beauty and distinction. The red dresses of the women who cluster round the fire on their stools give a glow of almost Eastern richness, and the walls have been toned by the turfsmoke to a soft brown that blends with the grey earth-color of the floor. Many sorts of fishing-tackle, and the nets and oilskins of the men, are hung upon the walls or among the open rafters; and right overhead, under the thatch, there is a whole cowskin from which they make pampooties.

Every article on these islands has an almost personal character, which gives this simple life, where all art is unknown, something of the artistic beauty of medieval life. The curaghs and spinning wheels, the tiny wooden barrels that are still much used in the place of earthenware, the homemade cradles, churns, and baskets, are all full of individuality, and being made from materials that are common here, yet to some extent peculiar to the island, they seem to exist as a natural link between the people and the world that is about them.

The simplicity and unity of the dress increases in another way the local air of beauty. The women wear red petticoats and jackets of the island wool stained with madder, to which they usually add a plaid shawl twisted round their chests and tied at the back. When it rains they throw another petticoat over their heads with the waistband round their faces, or, if they are young, they use a heavy shawl like those worn in Galway. Occasionally other wraps are worn, and during the thunderstorm I arrived in I saw several girls with men's waistcoats buttoned round their bodies. Their skirts do not come much below the knee, and show their powerful legs in the heavy indigo stockings with which they are all provided.

The men wear three colors: the natural wool, indigo, and a grey flannel that is woven of alternate threads of indigo and the natural wool. In Aranmor many of the younger men have adopted the usual fisherman's jersey, but I have only seen one on this island.

As flannel is cheap—the women spin the yarn from the wool of their own sheep, and it is then woven by a weaver in Kilronan for fourpence a yard—the men seem to wear an indefinite number of waistcoats and woollen drawers one over the other. They are usually surprised at the lightness of my own dress, and one old man I spoke to for a minute on the pier, when I came ashore, asked me if I was not cold with "my little clothes."

As I sat in the kitchen to dry the spray from my coat, several men who had seen me walking up came in to talk to me, usually murmuring on the threshold, "The blessing of God on this place," or some similar words.

The courtesy of the old woman of the house is singularly attractive, and though I could not understand much of what she said—she has no English—I could see with how much grace she motioned each visitor to a chair, or stool, according to his age, and said a few words to him till he drifted into our English conversation.

For the moment my own arrival is the chief subject of interest, and the men who come in are eager to talk to me.

Some of them express themselves more correctly than the ordinary peasant, others use the Gaelic idioms continually and substitute "he" or "she" for "it," as the neuter pronoun is not found in modern Irish.

A few of the men have a curiously full vocabulary, others know only the commonest words in English, and are driven to ingenious devices to express their meaning. Of all the subjects we can talk of war seems their favorite, and the conflict between America and Spain is causing a great deal of excitement. Nearly all the families have relations who have had to cross the Atlantic, and all eat of the flour and bacon that is brought from the United States, so they have a vague fear that "if anything happened to America," their own island would cease to be habitable.

Foreign languages are another favorite topic, and as these men are bilingual they have a fair notion of what it means to speak and think in many different idioms. Most of the strangers they see on the islands are philological students, and the people have been led to conclude that linguistic studies, particularly Gaelic studies, are the chief occupation of the outside world.

"I have seen Frenchmen, and Danes, and Germans," said one man, "and there does be a power of Irish books along with them, and they reading them better than ourselves. Believe me there are few rich men now in the world who are not studying the Gaelic."

They sometimes ask me the French for simple phrases, and when they have listened to the intonation for a moment, most of them are able to reproduce it with admirable precision.

When I was going out this morning to walk round the island with Michael, the boy who is teaching me Irish, I met an old man making his way down to the cottage. He was dressed in miserable black clothes which seemed to have come from the mainland, and was so bent with rheumatism that, at a little distance, he looked more like a spider than a human being.

Michael told me it was Pat Dirane, the storyteller old Máirtín had spoken of on the other island. I wished to turn back, as he appeared to be on his way to visit me, but Michael would not hear of it.

"He will be sitting by the fire when we come in," he said; "let you not be afraid, there will be time enough to be talking to him by and by."

He was right. As I came down into the kitchen some hours later old Pat was still in the chimney-corner, blinking with the turf smoke.

He spoke English with remarkable aptness and fluency, due, I believe, to the months he spent in the English provinces working at the harvest when he was a young man.

After a few formal compliments he told me how he had been crippled by an attack of the "old hin" (i.e., the influenza), and had been complaining ever since in addition to his rheumatism.

While the old woman was cooking my dinner he asked me if I liked stories, and offered to tell one in English, though he added, it would be much better if I could follow the Gaelic.

The Last Time

Desmond Hogan

THE LAST TIME I saw him was in Ballinasloe station, 1953, his long figure hugged into a coat too big for him. Autumn was imminent; the sky grey, baleful. A few trees had become grey too; God, my heart ached. The tennis court beyond, silent now, the river close, half-shrouded in fog. And there he was, Jamesy, tired, knotted, the doctor's son who took me out to the pictures once, courted me in the narrow timber seats as horns played in a melodramatic forties film.

Jamesy had half the look of a Mongol, half the look of an autistic child, blond hair parted like waves of water

DESMOND HOGAN (1950–) was born in Ballinasloe, County Galway. His debut novel, *The Ikon-Makers*, was published in 1976. In 1977 he received the Rooney Prize for Irish Literature. In 1980 he won the John Llewellyn Rhys Prize for his collection of short stories *Diamonds at the Bottom of the Sea*. In 1991 Hogan was awarded a place on the DAAD (German Academic Exchange) Berlin Artists' Programme fellowship, which enabled him to live in Berlin for an extended period of time. Hogan returned to Ireland in 1995, living in Clifden. He currently resides in a small village in County Kerry.

reeds, face salmon-color, long, the shade and color of autumnal drought. His father had a big white house on the perimeter of town—doors and windows painted as fresh as crocuses and lawns gloomy and yet blanched with perpetually new-mown grass.

In my girlhood I observed Jamesy as I walked with nuns and other orphans by his garden. I was an orphan in the local convent, our playfields stretching by the river at the back of elegant houses where we watched the nice children of town, bankers' children, doctors' children, playing. Maria Mulcahy was my name. My mother, I was told in later years, was a Jean Harlow–type prostitute from the local terraces. I, however, had hair of red which I admired in the mirror in the empty, virginal-smelling bathroom of the convent hall where we sat with children of doctors and bankers who had to pay three pence into the convent film show to watch people like Joan Crawford marry in bliss.

Jamesy was my first love, a distant love.

In his garden he'd be cutting hedges or reading books, a face on him like an interested hedgehog. The books were big and solemn-looking—like himself. Books like *War and Peace*, I later discovered.

Jamesy was the bright boy, though his father wanted him to do dentistry.

He was a problem child, it was well known. When I was seventeen I was sent to a draper's house to be a maid, and there I gathered information about Jamesy. The day he began singing "Bye Bye Blackbird" in the church, saying afterwards he was singing it about his grandmother who'd taken a boat one day, sailed down the river until the boat crashed over a weir and the woman drowned. Another day he was found having run away, sleeping on a red bench by the river where later we wrote our names, sleeping with a pet fox, for foxes were abundant that year.

Jamesy and I met first in the fair green. I was wheeling a child and in a check shirt he was holding a rabbit. The green was spacious, like a desert. *Duel in the Sun* was showing in town and the feeling between us was one of summer and space, the grass rich and twisted like an old nun's hair.

He smiled crookedly.

I addressed him.

"I know you!" I was blatant, tough. He laughed.

"You're from the convent."

"Have a sweet!"

"I don't eat them. I'm watching my figure!"

"Hold the child!"

I lifted the baby out, rested her in his arms, took out a rug and sat down. Together we watched the day slip, the sun steadying. I talked about the convent and he spoke about *War and Peace* and an uncle who'd died in the Civil War, torn apart by horses, his arms tied to their hooves.

"He was buried with the poppies," Jamesy said. And as though to remind us, there were sprays of poppies on the fair green, distant, distrustful.

"What age are you?"

"Seventeen! Do you see my rabbit?"

He gave it to me to hold. Dumbbells, he called it. There was a fall of hair over his forehead and by bold impulse I took it and shook it fast.

There was a smile on his face like a pleased sheep. "I'll meet you again," I said as I left, pushing off the pram as though it held billycans rather than a baby.

There he was that summer, standing on the bridge by the prom, sitting on a park bench or pawing a jaded copy of Turgenev's *Fathers and Sons.*

He began lending me books and under the pillow I'd read Zola's *Nana* or a novel by Marie Corelli, or maybe poetry by Tennyson. There was always a moon that summer—or a very red sunset. Yet I rarely met him, just saw him. Our relationship was blindly educational, little else. There at the bridge, a central point, beside which both of us paused, at different times, peripherally. There was me, the pram, and he in a shirt that hung like a king's cloak, or on cold days— as such there often were—in a jumper which made him look like a polar bear.

"I hear you've got a good voice," he told me one day.

"Who told you?"

"I heard."

"Well, I'll sing you a song." I sang. "Somewhere over the Rainbow," which I'd learnt at the convent.

Again we were in the green. In the middle of singing the song I realized my brashness and also my years of loneliness, destitution, at the hands of nuns who barked and crowded about the statue of the Infant Jesus of Prague in the convent courtyard like seals on a rock. They hadn't been bad, the nuns. Neither had the other children been so bad. But God, what loneliness there'd been. There'd been one particular tree there, open like a complaint, where I spent a lot of time surveying the river and the reeds, waiting for pirates or for some beautiful lady straight out of a Veronica Lake movie to come sailing up the river. I began weeping in the green that day, weeping loudly. There was his face which I'll never forget. Jamesy's face changed from blank idiocy, local precociousness, to a sort of wild understanding.

He took my hand.

I leaned against his jumper; it was a fawn color.

I clumsily clung to the fawn and he took me and I was aware of strands of hair, bleached by sun.

The Protestant church chimed five and I reckoned I should move, pushing the child ahead of me. The face of Jamesy Murphy became more intense that summer, his pink color changing to brown. He looked like a pirate in one of the convent film shows, tanned, ravaged.

Yet our meetings were just as few—and as autumn denuded the last of the cherry-colored leaves from a particular housefront on the other side of town Jamesy and I would meet by the river in the park—briefly, each day touching a new part of one another. An ankle, a finger, an ear lobe, something as ridiculous as that. I always had a child with me so it made things difficult.

Always too I had to hurry, often racing past closing shops.

There were Christmas trees outside a shop one day I noticed, so I decided Christmas was coming. Christmas was so unreal now, an event remembered from convent school, huge Christmas pudding and nuns crying. Always on Christmas Day nuns broke down crying, recalling perhaps a lost love or some broken-hearted mother in an Irish kitchen.

Jamesy was spending a year between finishing at school and his father goading him to do dentistry, reading books by Joyce now and Chekhov, and quoting to me one day—overlooking a garden of withered dahlias—Nijinsky's diaries. I took books from him about writers in exile from their countries, holding under my pillow novels by obscure Americans.

There were high clouds against a low sky that winter and the grotesque shapes of the Virgin in the alcove of the church, but against that monstrosity the romance was complete I reckon, an occasional mad moon, Lili Marlene on radio—memories of a war that had only grazed childhood—a peacock feather on an ascendancy-type lady's hat.

"Do you see the way that woman's looking at us," Jamesy said one day. Yes, she was looking at him as though he were a monster. His reputation was complete: a boy who was spoiled, daft, and an embarrassment to his parents. And there was I, a servant girl, talking to him. When she'd passed we embraced—lightly—and I went home, arranging to see him at the pictures the following night.

Always our meetings had occurred when I brushed past Jamesy with the pram. This was our first night out, seeing that Christmas was coming and that bells were tinkling on the radio; we'd decided we'd be bold. I'd sneak out at eight o'clock, having pretended to go to bed. What really enticed me to ask Jamesy to bring me to the pictures was the fact that he was wearing a new Aran sweater and that I heard the film was partly set in Marrakesh, a place that had haunted me ever since I had read a book about where a heroine and two heroes met their fatal end in that city.

So things went as planned until the moment when Jamesy and I were in one another's arms when the woman for whom I worked came in, hauled me off. Next day I was brought before Sister Ignatius. She sat like a robot in the

Spanish Inquisition. I was removed from the house in town and told I had to stay in the convent.

In time a job washing floors was found for me in Athlone, a neighboring town to which I got a train every morning. The town was a drab one, replete with spires.

I scrubbed floors, my head wedged under heavy tables: sometimes I wept. There were Sacred Heart pictures to throw light on my predicament but even they were of no avail to me; religion was gone in a convent hush. Jamesy now was lost; looking out of a window I'd think of him but like the music of Glenn Miller he was past. His hair, his face, his madness I'd hardly touched, merely fondled like a floating ballerina.

It had been a mute performance—like a circus clown. There'd been something I wanted of Jamesy which I'd never reached; I couldn't put words or emotions to it but now from a desk in London, staring into a Battersea dawn, I see it was a womanly feeling. I wanted love.

"Maria, you haven't cleaned the lavatory." So with a martyred air I cleaned the lavatory and my mind dwelt on Jamesy's pimples, ones he had for a week in September.

The mornings were drab and grey. I'd been working a year in Athlone, mind disconnected from body, when I learned Jamesy was studying dentistry in Dublin. There was a world of difference between us, a partition as deep as war and peace. Then one morning I saw him. I had a scarf on and a slight breeze was blowing and it was the aftermath of a sullen summer and he was returning to Dublin. He didn't look behind. He stared—almost at the tracks—like a fisherman at the sea.

I wanted to say something but my clothes were too drab; not the nice dresses of two years before, dresses I'd resurrected from nowhere with patterns of sea lions or some such thing on them.

"Jamesy Murphy, you're dead," I said—my head reeled.

"Jamesy Murphy, you're dead."

I travelled on the same train with him as far as Athlone. He went on to Dublin. We were in different carriages.

I suppose I decided that morning to take my things and move, so in a boat full of fat women bent on paradise I left Ireland.

I was nineteen and in love. In London through the auspices of the Sisters of Mercy in Camden Town I found work in an hotel where my red hair looked ravishing, sported over a blue uniform.

In time I met my mate, a handsome handy building contractor from Tipperary, whom I married—in the pleased absence of relatives—and with whom I lived in Clapham, raising children, he getting a hundred pounds a week, working seven days a week. My hair I carefully tended and wore heavy check shirts. We never went back to Ireland. In fact, we've never gone back to Ireland since I left, but occasionally, wheeling a child into the Battersea funfair, I was reminded of Jamesy, a particular strand of hair blowing across his face. Where was he? Where was the hurt and that face and the sensitivity? London was flooding with dark people and there at the beginning of the sixties I'd cross Chelsea Bridge, walk my children up by Cheyne Walk, sometimes waiting to watch a candle lighting. Gradually it became more real to me that I loved him, that we were active within a certain sacrifice. Both of us had been bare and destitute when we met. The two of us had warded off total calamity, total loss. "Jamesy!" His picture swooned; he was like a ravaged corpse in my head and the area between us opened; in Chelsea library I began reading books by Russian authors. I began loving him again. A snatch of Glenn Miller fell across the faded memory of colors in the rain, lights of the October fair week in Ballinasloe, Ireland.

The world was exploding with young people—protests against nuclear bombs were daily reported—but in me the nuclear area of the town where I'd worked returned to me.

Jamesy and I had been the marchers, Jamesy and I had been the protest! "I like your face," Jamesy once said to me. "It looks like you could blow it away with a puff."

In Chelsea library I smoked cigarettes though I wasn't supposed to, I read Chekhov's biography and Turgenev's biography—my husband minding the children—and tried to decipher an area of loss, a morning by the station, summer gone.

I never reached him; I just entertained him like as a child in an orphanage in the West of Ireland I had held a picture of Claudette Colbert under my pillow to remind me of glamor. The gulf between me and Jamesy narrows daily. I address him in a page of a novel, in a chip shop alone at night or here now, writing to you, I say something I never said before, something I've never written before.

I touch upon truth.

Going Home

Brian Moore

A FEW YEARS AGO on holiday in the west of Ireland I
came upon a field which faced a small strand and, beyond
it, the Atlantic Ocean. Ahead of me five cows raised their
heads and stared at the intruder. And then behind the cows
I saw a few stone crosses, irregular, askew as though they
had been thrown there in a game of pitch-and-toss. This
was not a field but a graveyard. I walked among the graves
and came to a path which led to the sandy shore below.
There, at the edge of this humble burial ground, was a

BRIAN MOORE (1921–1999) was born in Belfast, Northern
Ireland. He emigrated in 1948 to Canada where he worked as a
reporter for the *Montreal Gazette*. Moore published more than
twenty novels and was shortlisted for the Booker Prize three
times. His first novel, *The Lonely Passion of Judith Hearne* (1955),
remains among his most highly regarded. Subsequent novels
include *The Feast of Lupercal* (1957), *The Luck of Ginger Coffey*
(1960), *The Emperor of Ice Cream* (1965), *Catholics* (1972), *The
Mangan Inheritance* (1979), *Black Robe* (1985), *The Statement* (1995),
and *The Magician's Wife* (1997). Among his awards are The Gov-
ernor General of Canada's Award for Fiction in 1959. Brian
Moore died in 1999 at his home in Malibu, California, aged 77.

headstone unlike the others, a rectangular slab of white marble laid flat on the ground:

BULMER HOBSON
1883–1969

I stared at this name, the name of a man I had never known, yet familiar to me as a member of my family. I had heard it spoken again and again by my father in our house in Clifton Street in Belfast and by my uncle, Eoin MacNeill, when during school holidays I spent summers in his house in Dublin. For my uncle and my father, Bulmer Hobson was both a friend and in some sense a saint. A Quaker, he, like my uncle, devoted much of his life to the cause of Irish independence, becoming in the early years of this century an exemplary patriot whose nonviolent beliefs made our tribal animosities seem brutal and mean. That his body lay here in this small Connemara field, facing the ocean under a simple marker, was somehow emblematic of his life.

Proust says of our past: "It is a labor in vain to try to recapture it: all the efforts of our intellect are useless. The past is hidden somewhere outside its own domain in some material object which we never suspected. And it depends on chance whether or not we come upon it before we die."

I believe now that the "material object" was, for me, that gravestone in Connemara, a part of Ireland which I had never known in my youth. And as I stood staring at Bulmer Hobson's name, my past as a child and adolescent in Belfast surged up, vivid and importunate, bringing back a life which ended forever when I sailed to North Africa on a British troopship in the autumn of 1943.

There are those who choose to leave home vowing never to return and those who, forced to leave for economic reasons, remain in thrall to a dream of the land they left behind. And then there are those stateless wanderers who, finding the larger world into which they have stumbled vast, varied and exciting, become confused in their loyalties and lose their sense of home.

I am one of those wanderers. After the wartime years in North Africa and Italy, I worked in Poland for the United Nations, then emigrated to Canada, where I became a citizen before moving on to New York, and at last to California, where I have spent the greater part of my life.

And yet in all the years I have lived in North America I have never felt that it is my home. Annually, in pilgrimage, I go back to Paris and the French countryside and to London, the city which first welcomed me as a writer. And if I think of re-emigrating it is to France or England, not to the place where I was born.

For I know that I cannot go back. Of course, over the years I have made many return visits to my native Belfast. But Belfast, its configuration changed by the great air raids of the Blitz, its inner city covered with a carapace of flyovers, its new notoriety as a theater of violence, armed patrols and hovering helicopters, seems another city, a distant relative to that Belfast which in a graveyard in Connemara filled my mind with a jumbled kaleidoscope of images fond, frightening, surprising and sad.

—My pet canary is singing in its cage above my father's head as he sits reading *The Irish News* in the breakfast room of our house in Belfast—

—A shrill electric bell summons me to Latin class in the

damp, hateful corridors of St. Malachy's College. I have forgotten the declension and hear the swish of a rattan cane as I hold out my hand for punishment—

—In Fortstewart, where we spent our summer holidays, I have been all day on the sands, building an elaborate sand sculpture in hopes of winning the Cadbury contest first prize, a box of chocolates—

—Alexandra Park, where, a seven-year-old, I walk beside my sister's pram holding the hand of my nurse, Nellie Ritchie, who at that time I secretly believed to be my real mother—

—I hear the terrified squeal of a pig dragged out into the yard for butchery on my uncle's farm in Donegal—

—I stand with my brothers and sisters singing a ludicrous Marian hymn in St. Patrick's Church at evening devotions:

> *O Virgin pure, O spotless maid,*
> *We sinners send our prayers to thee,*
> *Remind thy Son that He has paid*
> *The price of our iniquity—*

—I hear martial music, as a regimental band of the British Army marches out from the military barracks behind our house. I see the shining brass instruments, the drummers in tiger-skin aprons, the regimental mascot, a large horned goat. Behind that imperial panoply long lines of poor recruits are marched through the streets of our native city to board ship for India, a journey from which many will never return—

—Inattentive and bored, I kneel at the Mass amid the stench of unwashed bodies in our parish church, where

80 percent of the female parishioners have no money to buy overcoats or hats and instead wear black woolen shawls which cover head and shoulders, marking them as "Shawlies," the poorest of the poor—

—We, properly dressed in our middle-class school uniforms sitting in a crosstown bus, move through the poor streets of Shankill and the Falls, where children without shoes play on the cobbled pavements—

—The front gates of the Mater Infirmorum Hospital, where my father, a surgeon, is medical superintendent. As he drives out of those gates, a man so poor and desperate that he will court minor bodily injury to be given a bed and food for a few days steps in front of my father's car—

—An evening curfew is announced following Orange parades and the clashes which invariably follow them. The curfew, my father says, is less to prevent riots than to stop the looting of shops by both Catholic and Protestant poor—

—Older now, I sit in silent teenage rebellion as I hear my elders talk complacently of the "Irish Free State" and the differences between the Fianna Fail and Fine Gael parties who compete to govern it. Can't they see that this Catholic theocratic "grocer's republic" is narrow-minded, repressive and no real alternative to the miseries and injustices of Protestant Ulster?—

—Unbeknownst to my parents I stand on Royal Avenue hawking copies of a broadsheet called *The Socialist Appeal,* although I have refused to join the Trotskyite party which publishes it. Belfast and my childhood have made me suspicious of faiths, allegiances, certainties. It is time to leave home—

The kaleidoscope blurs. The images disappear. The past is buried until, in Connemara, the sight of Bulmer Hobson's grave brings back those faces, those scenes, those sounds and smells which now live only in my memory. And in that moment I know that when I die I would like to come home at last to be buried here in this quiet place among the grazing cows.

The Lady with the Red Shoes
Ita Daly

THE WEST OF IRELAND, as every schoolboy knows, is
that part of the country to which Cromwell banished the
heretical natives after he had successfully brought the
nation to heel. Today, it is as impoverished and barren as
ever it was, bleak and lonesome and cowering from the savagery of the Atlantic which batters its coastline with all the
fury that it has gathered in over three thousand miles. But
the West of Ireland can also be heartbreakingly beautiful;
and on a fine April morning with the smell of gorse and
clover filling the air and the bees showing the only evidence
of industry in a landscape that is peopleless as far as the eye

ITA DALY (1945–) was born in County Leitrim. Her short
stories have won the Hennessy Literary Award and the Irish
Times short story competition, and are collected in *The Lady
with the Red Shoes* (1980). Oxford University Press published her
Irish Myths and Legends in 2000. Her novels include *Unholy
Ghosts* (1997), *All Fall Down* (1992), *Dangerous Fictions* (1991), *A
Singular Attraction* (1987) and *Ellen* (1986). She has written two
books for children, *Candy on the Dart* (1989) and *Candy and
Sharon Olé* (1991). She currently lives in Dublin with her husband
and daughter.

can see—on such a morning in the West of Ireland you can get a whiff of Paradise.

It is an irony which pleases me mightily that we as a family have such a strong attachment to the West. Our ancestors, you see, came over with Cromwell, foot soldiers who fought bravely and were rewarded generously and have never looked back since. And every Easter we leave Dublin and set out westwards where we spend a fortnight in McAndrews Hotel in North Mayo. It is a family tradition, started by my grandfather, and by now it has achieved a certain sacredness. Nothing is allowed to interfere with the ritual, and so when I married Judith one April day, some twenty-five years ago, it seemed quite natural that we should spend our honeymoon there. We have gone there every Easter since and if Judith has found it somewhat dull on occasion, she accepts gracefully a period of boredom in the knowledge that it gives me so much pleasure, while I in turn have been known to accompany her to Juan-les-Pins. An experience which, however, I have not been foolish enough to repeat.

McAndrews is one of the puzzles of the world. Built on the outskirts of Kilgory, looking down on the hamlet and on the sea, it dates back to the late nineteenth century. A large, square house, red-bricked and turreted, it is a reminder of the worst excesses of the Gothic revival, and every time I see its monstrous outline, lonely on the hill, my heart bounds and my pulse quickens. Nobody knows whether it was there before Kilgory and the village grew up around it or whether Kilgory was there first. But certainly it seems an odd place to have built a hotel, miles from a town, or a church, or even a beach. It is situated on a headland overlooking the Atlantic, but the cliffs are so steep and the sea so treacherous here that there is neither boating nor swimming available. Strange to build a hotel in such a place, stranger still that there have been enough eccentrics around to keep it in business for almost a century. My father, as a boy, used to arrive by train. The main line ran from Dublin to Westport and from there a branch line went to the hotel—not to Kilgory mark you, but to the actual hotel grounds. "Any guests for McAndrews?" the porters used to shout as one disembarked at Westport and was ushered on to a toy train with its three or four first-class carriages, to be shunted along the fifteen miles and deposited a stone's throw from the grand front door of McAndrews with its noble stone balustrade.

The toy station is still there, although nowadays the guests arrive by motor. I am always glad when I see my Daimler disappearing into the cavernous garages, and most of the other guests seem to experience a similar sense of relief, for though they arrive in motor cars, they continue thereafter on foot and the grounds and environs are delightfully free of petrol fumes. We are of a kind, McAndrews clientele, old-fashioned, odd perhaps; some would say snobbish. Well, if it is snobbish to exercise one's taste, then I admit that I am a snob. I do not like the bad manners, the insolence of shop assistants and taxi drivers which passes for egalitarianism in this present age; I resent chummy overtures from waiters who sometimes appear to restrain themselves with difficulty from slapping one on the back. I am irritated by cocktail bars and at a loss in the midst of all that bright and fatuous chatter. I like peace and quiet and reserve in my fellow man—decent reserve, which appears to be the raison d'être of McAndrews. I know most of my fellow guests' names—like me they have been coming here since they were children—yet I can rest assured that when I meet any of them again in any part of the hotel, I shall be spared all social intercourse apart from a civil word of greeting. Such respect for dignity and personal privacy is hard to come by in commercial establishments these days.

This year, Judith was ill and did not accompany me. To say that she was ill is something of an exaggeration, for if she had been, I would certainly not have left her. But she was somewhat under the weather, and as her sister was in Dublin from London, she decided to stay there with her while I went to Mayo alone. In truth, I was somewhat relieved, for I am only too aware of how difficult it must be for Judith, gay and outgoing, to be married to a dry stick like myself all these years. I am glad when she gets an opportunity to enjoy herself and I had no doubt that Eleanor and she would be much happier without my inhibiting presence. Still, I was going to miss her, for like many solitary people I am very dependent on the company of those few whom I love.

But the magic of McAndrews began to reassert itself as soon as I got down to breakfast the first morning and found Murphy, with his accustomed air of calm and dignity, presiding over the dining room. Murphy has been head waiter here for over thirty years now, although I always see him more as a butler, a loyal family retainer, rather than as a smart maître d'hôtel. His concern for each guest is personal and his old face is suffused with genuine pleasure when he sees you again each year. He came forward to greet me now. "Good morning, sir."

"Good morning, Murphy. Nice to see you again."

"And you, sir, always such a pleasure. I'm sorry Mrs. Montgomery will not be with us this year, sir?"

"Afraid not."

"Nevertheless, I hope you will have a pleasant stay. May I recommend the kippers this morning, sir? They are particularly good."

Such exchanges would be the extent of my intercourse with the world for the next fortnight—formal, impersonal, remote, and totally predictable. I have always found it a healing process, part of the total McAndrews experience, helping one to relax, unbend, find one's soul again.

I quickly re-established my routine, falling into it with the ease and gratitude one feels on putting on again an old and much-worn jacket. Breakfasts were latish but hearty, then a walk as far as the village and back. Afterwards an hour or two spent in the library in the delightful company of Boswell, a man to be enjoyed only in leisured circumstances—I never read him in Dublin. Lunch and an afternoon in a deck chair in the gardens, looking out to sea, dozing, dreaming, idling. After dinner another walk, this time more strenuous, perhaps two miles along the coast road and then back to McAndrews for a final glass of port followed by early bed with a good detective novel. The bliss of those days is hard to convey, particularly the afternoons, when it never seemed to rain. I would take my deck-chair and place it in a sheltered spot and sit, hour upon hour, and watch the Atlantic at its ceaseless labors. I'd watch as the light changed—from blue to green and from green to grey—until an occasional seagull would cut across my line of vision and I would raise my eyes and follow its soaring flight to the great vault of heaven. A couple of afternoons like that and things were back in perspective. The consciousness of one's encroaching age, the knowledge that one is regarded as a has-been, became less painful, and there, on the edge of the Atlantic, a peace began to make itself felt.

But then I have always been out of step with the world and even as a young man McAndrews was a retreat, a haven for me. However as I grow older and my unease increases, McAndrews becomes more precious. Here I can escape from all those aggressive young men with their extraordinary self-confidence and their scarlet-nailed women and their endless easy chatter. My son, Edward, who is married to a beautician—a profession which, I am assured, has some standing in this modern world—this son of mine tells me that my only problem is that I am a nasty old snob. This apparently puts me completely beyond the pale, and he views me as a pariah, almost as someone who should be put down. But we are all snobs of one variety or other, and what he really means is that my particular brand of snobbery has gone out of fashion. He has working-class friends and black friends, but no stupid friends; he would not dream of spending his holidays in such a bastion of privilege as McAndrews, but then neither would he think of going to the Costa Brava; he drinks pints of Guinness but abhors sweet wine. And he tells me that the difference between us is that he has discernment and that I am a snob.

The generation gap is what any modern sociologist would inelegantly and erroneously call it, for, as I have said, there has always been as big a gap between me and most of my own generation as there is between me and Edward's. It is a painful sensation, constantly feeling that the time is out of joint, although as I sit sipping sherry in McAndrews, in the pleasant expectation of a good dinner, I can laugh at my own foolishness and that of my son, and indeed, at the general idiocy of the human animal. This is what makes McAndrews so dear to me, but it is also what makes each leave-taking so difficult. I grow increasingly apprehensive before every return to the world, and as this holiday drew to a close and I finally sat waiting for dinner on the last evening, I was aware of my mounting nervousness and depression. I decided to console myself with that nectar of so many aging men—a bottle of vintage claret. Now as I sought Murphy's advice, I ignored, with unaccustomed recklessness, both the price and the knowledge that if I drank the whole bottle, I would undoubtedly spend a sleepless night. There were worse things than insomnia.

By dinnertime the light had changed outside and a soft blue opacity was flooding in from the Atlantic through the great windows of the dining room. This is the Irish twilight, most beautiful of times and that part of the day I missed most during those few years I spent in West Africa as a young man. It is a time that induces a half-willful melancholia—helped no doubt by the glass in one's hand—and in McAndrews they respect this mood, for the curtains are never drawn nor the lights switched on until darkness finally descends. As I moved through the flickering pools of yellow light—for there were many diners already present and many candles lit—I was struck again by the solemnity of the room. Years and years of ritual have given it a churchlike quiet, a hint of the ceremony and seriousness with which eating is invested by both guests and staff. I took my usual seat against the wall, facing out towards sea, and as Murphy murmured, priestlike, over the wine, we were both startled by a raised and discordant voice. "Waiter, come here please."

Together we turned towards the voice, both acutely conscious of the solecism that had been committed in referring to Murphy as "Waiter." The offender was sitting about six feet away at a small table in the middle of the room. It was an unpopular table, unprotected, marooned under the main chandelier, seldom occupied except when the hotel was very busy. I guessed now that some underling, flustered by the novelty of the situation, had forgotten himself to such an extent as to usher this person to it without first consulting Murphy. And the arrival of this new diner *was* a novelty. She was not a resident, which was odd in itself, for McAndrews has never been the sort of place to seek out a casual trade; then she was alone, unescorted, a sight which was not only odd, but simply not done: ladies, one feels, do not dine alone in public. But the most striking thing of all about our newcomer was her appearance. She was in her fifties, maybe sixty, with hair and dress matching, both of an indeterminate pink. She wore spectacles which were decorated with some kind of stones along the wings. These shone and sparkled as she moved her head, but no more brightly than her teeth, which were of an amazing and American brightness. She flashed them up at

Murphy now, and as he shied away from their brilliance, I could see that for once he was discomposed. But Murphy is a gentleman and within seconds he had himself again in hand. Stiffening his back, he bowed slightly in the direction of the teeth. "Madam?" he enquired, with dignity.

"Could I have a double Scotch on the rocks, and I'd like a look at the menu." Her voice had that familiarity which so many aspects of American life have for Europeans who have never even crossed the Atlantic. I don't think I have ever met an American, but I have a great fondness for their television thrillers, and I immediately identified the voice as a New York voice, tough New York, like so many of my favorite villains. Proud of my detective work, I sat back to listen.

The whiskey had appeared with that speed to which we McAndrews guests are accustomed, and if Murphy disapproved of this solitary diner, his training was too perfect to even suggest it. He hovered beside her now, solicitously, as she studied the menu, and as she turned it over and turned it back again I noticed her face grow tight and apprehensive. I should say here that McAndrews does not have a menu in the usual commercial sense of that word. Mrs. Byrne, who has been cooking there for the past thirty years, is an artist, and it would offend her artistic sensibility, and indeed equally displease the guests, if she were asked to produce the commonplace, vast à la carte vulgarity that one finds in so many dining places today. For festive occasions she will prepare a classic dish in the French tradition, and otherwise she keeps us all happy cooking simple but superb dishes using the local fish and meat and the vegetables which grow a couple of hundred yards away. She is a wonder certainly, but I can perfectly understand that one used to the meaningless internationalism of the modern menu might find Mrs. Byrne's handwritten and modest proposals something of a puzzle. One would look in vain for the tired Entrecôte Chasseur or the ubiquitous Sole Bonne Femme in this dining room and be somewhat at a loss when faced with the humble, boiled silverside of beef followed by stewed damsons with ginger.

I could see that this was precisely the position in which our lady diner now found herself. She toyed with the piece of paper and looked up helplessly at Murphy. Murphy coughed encouragingly behind a genteel hand and began, "Perhaps Madam, I could recommend tonight the—." But she gathered her shoulders together and threw back her head. "No, you could not, waiter. I know exactly what I want." Her voice had taken on an added stridency. "I want a fillet mignon with a green salad. Surely a place like this can produce that—huh?"

"It is not on the menu, Madam, but certainly if that is what you require, we can arrange it." I thought I noticed a hint of disapproval in Murphy's silky tones.

"Yeah, that's what I want. Nothing to start and I want the steak medium rare, and I mean medium rare. All you Irish overcook meat."

I thought for a moment that Murphy was going to lose control, that years of training and polish would at last begin to give way before this latest onslaught of rudeness, but again he recovered himself. For a moment he paused over his order and then looked up again and said, still politely, "And to drink Madam, would you like something?" The lady looked at him, genuinely puzzled as she held up her whiskey glass. "I've gotten it already—remember?" It was now Murphy's turn to look puzzled and I could see him struggling mentally before the implication of her remark became clear to him. This extraordinary person intended to drink whiskey with her fillet mignon!

As I watched my fellow diner I wondered how on earth she had ever found her way to McAndrews. It was not a fashionable spot, not the sort of place that attracted tourists. There was a hideous motel only ten miles away, much smarter than McAndrews, flashing neon lights, full of Americans, supplying what they called an ensemble for the gratification of their guests. Surely this woman would have been much more at home in such a place? But as I studied her, I began to realize that this strange creature was actually impressed by McAndrews. I was sure now that she hadn't accidentally happened upon it as I had at first surmised, but that for some unknown reason she had chosen it deliberately. And I saw too that her apparent rudeness was no more than awkwardness, an effort to hide her awe and inexperience in such surroundings. My daughter-in-law—the beautician—when she visited me here once gave a display of genuine rudeness, authentic because it was based on contempt, for Murphy, for me, for our kind of world. She shouted at Murphy because she saw him as an inefficient old fogey. But he didn't impinge at all on her world and was only a nuisance to her because he did not mix her cocktail in the correct proportions. This woman however was different, although I saw that Murphy didn't think so—indeed whereas he was prepared to make excuses for Helen, as one of the family, I could tell that he had put up with as much as he was going to from an outsider. As the waiter placed the steak in front of her, Murphy approached, disapproval in every line of his stately person. "Medium rare, as you required," he said, and even I, sitting some distance away, drew back from the sting of his contempt.

Other guests were taking notice now, attracted perhaps by Murphy's slightly raised voice, a unique occurrence in this dining-room. I could feel a current of mild disapproval beginning to circulate and I saw that the lady was noticing something too. She was looking discomfited but bravely she took up her knife and fork and tucked in her chin. I was beginning to admire her pluck.

Decency demanded that I leave her some privacy to eat so reluctantly I looked away. Soon, I was glad to see, the other guests lost interest in her, and when after a safe interval I glanced back at her table, she had finished her meal and was wiping her mouth with an air of well-being and relaxation. It must have been a satisfactory fillet mignon. When Murphy brought the menu again, she actually smiled at him. "No, no," she said waving it away, "nothing more for me. We women have to watch our figures—eh?" And as she glanced at him archly, I thought for an awful moment that she was going to dig him in the ribs. Murphy looked at her coldly, making no effort to return her smile. "Very well, Madam." The words hung between them and as she sensed his unfriendliness, indeed hostility, the smile, still awkward upon her lips, became transfixed in an ugly grimace. "I guess you'd better bring me another Scotch." Defeat was now beginning to edge out defiance in her voice. She grasped her drink when it arrived, and gulped it, as a drowning man gulps air. This seemed to steady her somewhat and taking another, slower sip, she drew out a cigarette from her bag and lit it. It was then that she discovered, just as Murphy was passing on his way towards my table, that there was no ashtray. "Excuse me," she sounded embarrassed, "could you bring me an ashtray please?" Murphy turned slowly in his tracks. He looked at her in silence for fully five seconds. "I am sorry, Madam,"—and it seemed to me now that the whole dining room was listening to his even, slightly heightened tones—"I am sorry, but our guests do not smoke in the dining room." In essence this is true, it being accepted among the guests that tobacco is not used in here—a measure of their consideration for each other as smoke fumes might lessen someone's enjoyment of an excellent meal. I thoroughly approve of this unwritten rule—it seems to me to be eminently civilized—but I know well that on occasions, people, newcomers for example, have smoked in McAndrews dining-room, and Murphy, though perhaps disapproving, has never demurred. I looked at him now in amazement and maybe he caught my expression of surprise, for he added, "Coffee is served in the blue sitting room, Madam, there are ashtrays there. However, if you'd prefer it, I can—" The woman stood up abruptly, almost colliding with Murphy. Her face and neck were flooded with an ugly red color and she seemed to be trying to push him away. "No, not at all, I'll have the coffee," and she blundered blindly towards the door. It seemed a long, long journey.

I finished my cheese and followed her thoughtfully into the sitting room. All evening something had been niggling me, something about that voice. I have a very sensitive ear I believe—I am rather proud of it—and although, as I had noticed, this woman spoke with an American accent, there was some underlying non-American quality about it. Something familiar but different about those vowels and th's. Now as I sat and lit my cigar, I realized what it was— it was so obvious that I had missed it until now. Her voice, of course, was a local voice, a North Mayo voice with that thick and doughy consistency that I was hearing around me since I had come down. It had become Americanized, almost completely so, but to my ear its origins were clear. I could swear that that woman had been born within ten miles of this very hotel.

We both sipped our coffee, the tinkle of coffee spoons falling between us. I watched her as she sat alone, isolated and tiny in the deep recess of the bay window, looking out at the darkening gardens. Beyond, there were still some streaks of light coming from the sea, and I knew that down below on the rocks the village children would be gathering their final bundles of seaweed before heading off home to bed. The seaweed is sold to the local factory where it is turned into fertilizer of some kind and the people here collect it assiduously, sometimes whole families working together, barefooted, for the salt water rots shoe-leather. Even the little ones often have hard and calloused feet, sometimes with ugly cuts. Life is still hard in the West of Ireland. I looked across at my lady—*her* feet were encased in red high-heeled shoes with large platform soles. Her face, as she gazed out unseeing, was sad now, sad and crumpled-looking. I recalled again her voice, and as we sat there, drinking our coffee, I suddenly knew without any shadow of doubt what she was doing there. I knew *her* intimately—her life was spread out in front of me. I could see her as a little girl, living nearby in some miserable cottage. Maybe, when I was out walking as a child with my Mama, I had even passed her, not noticing the tattered little girl who stood in wonder, staring at us. McAndrews must have been a symbol to her, a world of wealth and comfort, right there on the doorstep of her own poverty-stricken existence. Perhaps she had even worked in the hotel as a maid, waiting to save her fare to America, land of opportunity. And in America, had she been lonely, frightened by that alien place, so different from her own Mayo? Had she wept herself to sleep many nights, sick for a breath of home? But she had got on, sent money back, and always, all those years, she had kept her dream intact: one day she would return home to Kilgory, a rich American lady, and she would go in to McAndrews Hotel, not as a maid this time but as a guest. She would order a fine dinner and impress everyone with her clothes and her accent and her wealth.

She sat now, a rejected doll in her pink dress and red shoes, for tonight she had seen that dream disintegrate like candy floss. I wanted to go to her, to tell her, explain to her that it didn't matter any more—the world itself was disintegrating. She should realize that places like McAndrews weren't important any longer, people only laughed at them now. She had no need to be saddened, for she, and all those other little Irish girls who had spent their days washing other people's floors and cooking other people's meals, they would inherit the earth. The wheel had come round full circle.

Of course I didn't approach her, I finished my coffee and went straight to bed thinking how the world is changing, my world, her world. Soon McAndrews itself will be gone.

But for me, this landscape has been caught forever—caught and defined by its heroine, the lady with the red shoes. Of course, you, on reading this, are going to see me as a sentimental old codger, making up romantic stories about strangers, because I am lonely and have nothing better to do. But I know what I know.

The Stoat

John McGahern

I WAS FOLLOWING a two iron I had struck just short of
the green when I heard the crying high in the rough grass
above the fairway. The clubs rattled as I climbed towards
the sound, but it did not cease, its pitch rising. The light
of water from the inlet was blinding when I climbed out
of the grass, and I did not see the rabbit at once, where it
sat rigidly still on a bare patch of loose sand, crying. I was

JOHN MCGAHERN (1943–2006) was born in Dublin but
moved to Leitrim as a child. His novels include *The Barracks*
(1963), *The Dark* (1965), *The Leavetaking* (1975), *The Pornographer*
(1980), *Amongst Women* (1990), and *That They May Face the Rising Sun* (2001). His short story collections include *Nightlines*
(1970) and *High Ground* (1985), which were brought together in
The Collected Stories (1992). Among his most recent published
works is *Memoir* (2005). He received multiple awards including
the Æ Award (1962), Macaulay Fellowship (1964), The Arts
Council/An Chomhairle Éalaíon Award (1980), The Irish
American Foundation Award (1985), Chevalier d'Ordre des Arts
et des Lettres (1989), The Irish Times/Aer Lingus Literary
Award (1990), and the Prix Étranger Ecureuil (1994). McGahern
died on March 30, 2006.

standing over the rabbit when I saw the grey body of the stoat slithering away like a snake into the long grass.

The rabbit still did not move, but its crying ceased. I saw the wet slick of blood behind its ear, the blood pumping out on the sand. It did not stir when I stooped. Never before did I hold such pure terror in my hands, the body trembling in a rigidity of terror. I stilled it with a single stroke. I took the rabbit down with the bag of clubs and left it on the edge of the green while I played out the hole. Then as I crossed to the next tee I saw the stoat cross the fairway following me still. After watching two simple shots fade away into the rough, I gave up for the day. As I made my way back to the cottage my father rented every August, twice I saw the stoat, following the rabbit still, though it was dead.

All night the rabbit must have raced from warren to warren, the stoat on its trail. Plumper rabbits had crossed the stoat's path but it would not be deflected; it had marked down this one rabbit to kill. No matter how fast the rabbit raced, the stoat was still on its trail, and at last the rabbit sat down in terror and waited for the stoat to slither up and cut the vein behind the ear. I had heard it crying as the stoat was drinking its blood.

My father was reading the death notices on the back of the *Independent* on the lawn of the cottage. He always read the death notices first, and then, after he had exhausted the news and studied the ads for teachers, he'd pore over the death notices again.

"Another colleague who was in Drumcondra the same year as myself has gone to his reward," he said when he looked up. "A great fullback poor Bernie was, God rest him."

I held up the rabbit by way of answer.

"Where did you get that?"

"A stoat was killing it on the links."

"That's what they do. Why did you bring it back?"

"I just brought it. The crying gave me a fright."

"What will we cook for dinner? You know Miss McCabe is coming tonight?"

"Not the poor rabbit anyhow. There's lamb chops and cheese and wine and salad."

My father had asked me to come to Strandhill because of Miss McCabe. They'd been seeing one another for several months and had arranged to spend August at the ocean. They seemed to have reached some vague, timid understanding that if the holiday went well they'd become engaged before they returned to their schools in September. At their age, or any age, I thought their formality strange, and I an even stranger chaperon.

"Why do you want me to come with you?" I had asked.

"It'd look more decent—proper—and I'd be grateful if you'd come. Next year you'll be a qualified doctor with a life of your own."

I had arranged to do postgraduate work for my uncle, a surgeon in Dublin, when my father pleaded for this last summer. I would golf and study, he would read the *Independent* and see Miss McCabe.

The summer before he had asked me, "Would you take it very much to heart if I decided to marry again?"

"Of course I wouldn't. Why do you ask?"

"I was afraid you might be affronted by the idea of

another woman holding the position your dear mother held."

"Mother is dead. You should do exactly as you want to."

"You have no objections, then?"

"None whatever."

"I wouldn't even think of going ahead if you'd any objections."

"Well, you can rest assured, then. I have none. Have you someone in mind?"

"No, I don't," he answered absently.

I put it aside as some wandering whim until several weeks later when he offered me a sheet of paper on which was written in his clear, careful hand: *Teacher, fifty-two. Seeks companionship. View marriage.* "What do you think of it?" he asked.

"I think it's fine." Dismay cancelled a sudden wild impulse to roar with laughter.

"I'll send it off, then, so."

After about a month he showed me the response. A huge pile of envelopes lay on his desk. I was amazed. I had no idea that so much unfulfilled longing wandered around in the world. Replies came from nurses, housekeepers, secretaries, childless widows, widows with small children, house owners, car owners, pensioners, teachers, civil servants, a policewoman, and a woman who had left at twenty years of age to work at Fords of Dagenham who wanted to come home. The postman inquired slyly if the school was seeking a new assistant, and the woman who ran the post office said in a faraway voice that if we were looking for a housekeeper she had a relative who might be interested.

"I hope they don't steam the damn letters. This country is on fire with curiosity," he said.

Throughout the winter I saw much of him because he had to meet many of the women in Dublin though he had to go to Cork and Limerick and Tullamore as well. In hotel lounges he met them, hiding behind a copy of the *Roscommon Herald.*

"You've never in your life seen such a collection of wrecks and battleaxes as I've had to see in the last few months," he said, a cold night in late March after he had met the lady from Dagenham in the Ormond. "You'd need to get a government grant before you could even think of taking some of them on."

"Do you mean in appearance or as people?"

"All ways," he said despairingly. "I have someone who seems a decent person, at least compared to what I've seen," and for the first time he told me about Miss McCabe.

Because of these interviews I was under no pressure to go home for Easter and I spent it with my uncle in Dublin. I wasn't able to resist telling him, "My father's going to get married."

"You must be joking. You'd think boring one poor woman in a lifetime would be enough."

"He's gone about it in a curious way. He's put an ad in the papers."

"An ad!" Suddenly my uncle became convulsed with laughter and was hardly able to get words out. "Did he get . . . replies?"

"Bundles. He's been interviewing them."

"Bundles . . . God help us all. This is too much."

"Apparently, he's just found someone. A schoolteacher in her forties."

"Have you seen this person?"

"Not yet. I'm supposed to see her soon."

"My God, if you hang round long enough you see everything."

My uncle combed his fingers through his long greying hair. He was a distinguished man and his confidence and energy could be intimidating. "At least, if he does get married, it'll get him off your back."

"He's all right," I replied defensively. "I'm well used to him by now."

I met Miss McCabe in the lobby of the Ormond Hotel, a lobby that could have been little different to the many lobbies he had waited in behind a copy of the *Roscommon Herald*. They sat in front of me, very stiffly and properly, like two well-dressed, well-behaved children seeking adult approval. She was small and frail and nervous, a nervousness that extended, I suspected, well beyond the awkwardness and unease of the whole contrived meeting. There was something about her—a waif-like sense of decency—that was at once appealing and troubling. Though old, she was like a girl, in love with being in love a whole life long without ever settling on any single demanding presence until this late backward glance fell on my bereft but seeking father.

"Well, what was your impression?" he asked me when we were alone.

"I think Miss McCabe is a decent, good person," I said uncomfortably.

"You have . . . no objections, then?"

"None."

We had been here a week. I had seen Miss McCabe three or four times casually. She looked open-eyed and happy. She stayed in the Seaview Hotel beside the salt baths on the ocean front and went for walks along the shore with my father. They had lunches and teas together. Tonight she was coming to the house for the first time. In all his years in the world my father had never learned to cook, and I offered to take care of the dinner.

She wore a long blue printed dress, silver shoes, and silver pendants, like thin elongated pears, hung from her ears. Though she praised the food she hardly ate at all and took only a few sips from the wine glass. My father spoke of schools and curricula and how necessary it was to get to the sea each August to rid oneself of staleness before starting back into the new school year, and her eyes shone as she followed every heavy word.

"You couldn't be more right. The sea will always be wonderful," she said.

It seemed to discomfort my father, as if her words belonged more to the sea and air than to his own rooted presence.

"What do you think?" he asked predictably when he returned from leaving her back to the Seaview.

"I think she is a very gentle person."

"Do you think she has her feet on the ground?"

"I think you are very lucky to have found her," I said. The way he looked at me told me he was far from convinced that he had been lucky.

The next morning he looked at me in a more dissatisfied

manner still when a girl came from the Seaview to report that Miss McCabe had a mild turn during the night. A doctor had seen her. She was recovering and resting in the hotel and wanted to see my father. The look on his face told me that he was more than certain now that she was not near rooted enough.

"Will you come with me?" he asked.

"It is yourself she wants to see."

When he got back from the hotel he was agitated. "She's all right," he said. "She had a mild heart attack. She still thinks we'll get engaged at the end of the month."

"I thought that was the idea."

"It was. If everything went well," he said with emphasis.

"Did you try to discuss it with her?"

"I tried. I wasn't able. All she thinks of is our future. Her head is full of plans."

"What are you going to do?"

"Clear out," he said. "There is no other way."

As if all the irons were suddenly being truly struck and were flowing from all directions to the heart of the green, I saw that my father had started to run like the poor rabbit. He would have been better off if he could have tried to understand something, even though it would get him off nothing. Miss McCabe was not alone in her situation.

"Where'll you go to?" I asked.

"Home, of course. What are you going to do?"

"I'll stay here a while longer. I might go to Dublin in a few days."

"What if you run into her and she asks about me?"

"I'll tell her you had to go home. How soon are you going?"

"As soon as I get the stuff into the boot of the car."

Because I was ashamed of him I carried everything he wanted out to the car.

"I hope you don't mind," he said as he prepared to drive away.

"No. I don't mind."

I watched the car climb the hill. When it had gone out of sight I had the clear vision again of hundreds of irons being all cleanly struck and flowing from every direction into the very heart of the green.

All night the rabbit must have raced from warren to warren, the stoat on its trail. Plumper rabbits had crossed the stoat's path but it would not be deflected; it had marked down this one rabbit to kill. No matter how fast the rabbit raced, the stoat was still on its trail, and at last the rabbit sat down in terror and waited for the stoat to slither up and cut the vein behind the ear. I had heard it crying as the stoat was drinking its blood.

The Saucer of Larks

Brian Friel

THEY DROVE the first ten miles in silence. Once, at a point where the main road veered inland and they followed a narrower track that ran along the rim of the Atlantic, the Sergeant took his pipe from between his teeth and said, "This is all my kingdom as far as you can see," and Herr Grass said "Yes?" in such a way that the Sergeant was not sure if the German had understood him. He had replied

BRIAN FRIEL (1929–) was born in County Tyrone in Northern Ireland. Friel is regarded as one of Ireland's most prominent playwrights. His plays have premiered at theatrical venues such as the Abbey Theatre, London's West End, and Broadway. His first major play, *Philadelphia, Here I Come!* was the hit of the 1964 Dublin Theatre Festival. In 1972 he was elected as a member of the Irish Academy of Letters. *Translations*, one of his most celebrated pieces, was awarded the Ewart-Biggs Peace Prize in 1981. *Dancing at Lughnasa*, his most successful play to date, received three Tony Awards in 1992 (including Best Play). His short story collections include *A Saucer of Larks* (1962) and *The Gold in the Sea* (1966). Friel is a member of Aosdána, and lives in County Donegal.

"Yes?" to so many things that the Sergeant had said that morning—questions about the work they were on and other parts of the country they had still to visit—that the old policeman resolved once more that he would keep quiet and enjoy the sun. It pleased him that the two in the rear seat, Guard Burke, his assistant, and the other German, Herr Henreich, also found conversation too difficult.

The Sergeant was a Cavan man and a garrulous man. He had been twenty-six years in Donegal but there were times when its beauty still shocked him; as on this spring morning with the sea spreading out and away into the warm sky and a high, fresh sun taking winking lights out of the granite-covered countryside. He just had to comment on it.

"Dammit, it's lovely, isn't it, eh? God Himself above you and the best of creation all round you. D'you know, only that the missus is buried away down in the midlands, I wouldn't mind being laid to rest anywhere along the coast here myself."

"Yes?" said Herr Grass. He was young and clean and polite.

"Not that it matters a curse, I suppose, where they put you when the time comes. But it would be nice to have the sea near you and the birds above you, wouldn't it?" He stole a glance at the German's face. "And you wouldn't be disturbed every ten minutes with funerals crawling past you— I seen them myself years ago when I was stationed in Dublin. Every ten minutes they come; everyone looking sad and miserable. I'm telling you: everything's dead in them places. Once they put you in them big cemeteries, you're finished, all right."

"Very depressing indeed, Sergeant," said Guard Burke from behind, hoping to match his Sergeant's mood.

"But do you see what I mean about being buried out here in the wilds?" The Sergeant was warming up. "Out here, it's not the same at all, Burke. Out here, man, you still have life all around you. Dammit, there's so much good life around you, you haven't a chance to be really dead!"

"Very pretty. Very pretty," said Herr Grass.

"A grand spot," echoed Burke.

The Sergeant, who was not too sure that he had made himself clear, stuck his pipe between his teeth again.

The car went cautiously because the surface of the road was bad. Houses became fewer. Small quilts of farms lost heart in their struggle against obdurate, peaty, rocky earth and disappeared altogether. Then there was nothing but barren bogland and here and there an occasional gnarled tree, its back to the ocean, its tortuous arms outstretched to the shelter of the interior. A long, thin promontory of about three miles in length shot out at right angles to the coast line.

"That's where we're heading," said the Sergeant. "Out to the tip of yon neck. That's where your man's buried. Turn right when we come to the white rock below."

"The road . . . ?" began Herr Grass.

"Who would want a road out to a place like that?" said the Sergeant. "There's a sort of a track, as far as I remember. Drive on, man!"

They drove out along the narrow strip as far as they could but halfway the track became potted with rabbit holes. Herr Grass stopped suddenly.

"It is safer and quicker to walk, perhaps," he said.

"Whatever you say," said the Sergeant. "A bit of a walk will take some of the mutton from beneath this shirt of mine."

"Yes?" said Herr Grass.

"Just a manner of talking," mumbled the Sergeant.

Herr Henreich, who had not spoken up to this, said something in German to Herr Grass and Herr Grass gave him the keys of the car. He then went back to the boot, opened it and took out a spade and a large white canvas bag which he folded neatly and placed under his arm. Herr Grass joined him and they talked rapidly together.

"Can I give you a hand there?" called the Sergeant.

"Yes?" said Herr Grass.

"Christ!" said the Sergeant softly to himself; then to Guard Burke, "Come on, man, We'll lead the way."

They followed the track which ran up the middle of the lean peninsula. At times it broadened into a road, wide enough to carry a car and then it would unexpectedly taper into a thin path and vanish into a bunker of sand.

"The man that battered out this route must never have sobered," panted the Sergeant.

Burke was glad of the opening.

"What do you make of them?" he whispered confidentially.

"Make of what?"

"Them German fellas."

"What do you mean, what do I make of them? They're doing a job of work here, a duty, just as they're doing the same duty all round the country. And we're here to see that everything's carried out legally and properly. That's what I make of them." And to show Burke that he was not to be drawn into any narrow criticism of the foreigners, he turned round and shouted back to the men behind, "Do you see the wee specks in the water away south there below the island? That's the men from Gola Island shooting their lobster pots. The lobsters are exported to France and to Switzerland and to England—aye, and to your own country too. So when you go home, you can say that you seen where they come from."

"Yes?" called Herr Grass against the wind.

"What did he say?" asked the Sergeant.

"'Yes?'" mimicked Burke accurately.

"I'm beginning to think he says that just to annoy me," said the Sergeant.

Half a mile from the end of the promontory, the path dipped sharply into a miniature valley, a saucer of green grass bordered by yellow sand dunes and the promontory itself ended in a high, blunt hill which broke the Atlantic wind. For a few seconds after they entered the valley, their ears still heard the rush of the breeze and they were still inclined to call to one another. Then they became aware of the silence and then, no sooner were they hushed by it, than they heard the larks, not a couple or a dozen or a score, but hundreds of them, all invisible against the blue heat of the sky, an umbrella of music over this tiny world below.

"God, isn't it grand, eh?" said the Sergeant. He dropped clumsily on the grass and screwed his face up in an effort to see the birds against the light. Guard Burke sat beside him and opened the collar of his tunic. Herr Grass and Herr Henreich stood waiting. "Dammit, could you believe that there are places like this still in the world, eh? D'you know, there are men would give fortunes for a place like this. Fortunes. And what would they do if they got it? What would they do?"

"What, Sergeant?" asked Burke dutifully.

"They would destroy it! That's what they would do! Dig it up and flatten it out and build houses on it and ring it round with cement. Kill it. That's what they would do. Kill it. Didn't I see them myself when I was stationed in Dublin years ago, making an arse of places like Malahide and Skerries and Bray. That's what I mean. Kill it! Slaughter it!"

Herr Grass had a notebook and pencil in his hand.

"This is Glennafushog?"

"Glenn-na-fuiseog," said the Sergeant, pronouncing the Gaelic name properly. "It means the valley of the larks. You need to be careful where you walk here: you might stand on a nest and crush it. Listen to them, man! Listen to them!" He tilted his head sideways and his mouth dropped open and his big, fleshy chest rose and fell silently. Grass and Henreich and Burke looked around them casually. After a few minutes, he gathered himself together and when he spoke, he avoided Grass's face.

"Herr Grass," he began, "I suppose you never done an irregular thing in your life?"

"Yes?"

"What I mean is"—the old policeman sought earnestly for the right words—"I suppose you never did a wrong thing . . . did something that was against orders?"

"Disobey?"

The Sergeant did not like the word. He hesitated before accepting it. "Aye . . . aye . . . disobey . . . that will do. Disobey. Did you ever disobey your superiors, Herr Grass?"

The German considered the question seriously. "No . . ." he replied slowly. Then with finality, "No."

Burke was watching his Sergeant keenly.

"Neither did I neither," said the Sergeant. "Never. But there are times, I think, when it might not be such a bad thing to . . . to . . ." He saw Burke watching him and he looked away. "There are times when a man could overlook orders . . . forget about them."

"Overlook?" said Herr Grass.

The Sergeant got to his feet and faced the German.

"I'm going to ask you to do something." His breath came in short puffs and he spoke quickly. "Leave that young lad here. Don't dig him up."

Herr Grass stiffened.

"Let him lie here where he has all that's good in God's earth around about him. He has been here for the past eighteen years; he's part of the place by now. Leave him in it. Let him rest in peace."

"My orders are . . ."

"Who's to know, I ask you? Who's to tell what happened? I'll fill up whatever forms you have from your government and Burke here will cause no trouble. It will be a private thing between the four of us. No one will be a bit the wiser."

"It is getting late. We must return to Dublin today," said Herr Grass.

"You don't understand me," said the Sergeant. "I'm asking you not to touch this grave—this one. Do you understand that?" He raised his voice and said each word deliberately: "Do not touch this grave. I will not tell any one.

Burke here will not tell. I will sign your papers." He wheeled to his assistant. "Burke, you try him. He doesn't understand me: it's the way I talk."

"I understand," said Herr Grass. "But I have orders to obey."

The four men stood awkwardly, looking at one another. The Sergeant's face which had been animated and tense while he was pleading, held its concentration until the flush of anger at Grass's refusal drained out of it. Then it went flabby and a nerve under his right eye twitched spasmodically. In the silence that followed, the heat of the sun poured down on them in waves. The air was a great void of warmth around them. Gradually the emptiness was filled again by the larks, slowly at first, then more and more of them until the saucer-valley shimmered with their singing.

The Sergeant's weighty body sagged in his uniform. He looked across the valley at the blunt hill.

"He was a young airman from Hamburg." He spoke limply. "And he crashed into that stump of a hill over there. It was a night in the summer of '42 and his plane was burned to ashes."

Herr Grass consulted his notebook.

"First Sergeant Werner Endler," he read.

"He was dead when I got here. And buried. The fishermen found him about fifty yards from the plane. They made a grave and laid him to rest in it before priest or any one came because it was weather like this and the lad was badly burned." He rubbed his hands down the legs of his trousers to dry the sweat off them.

"The exact position? Is it marked?"

"I know where it is," said the Sergeant. "Come on."

He launched himself forward into the mass of heat and left the others to follow him.

The grave, a mound of grass sprinkled with wild May flowers, lay at the foot of the blunt hill. Herr Henreich opened it and put what remains he found into the white canvas bag. Then he closed the grave again and smoothed over the clay with his hands, leaving the place tidier then he had found it. While the exhumation was being done, the Sergeant paced up and down a few feet from where the Germans were working and Burke went over the dunes to relieve himself. The whole job was completed within twenty minutes.

"I think that is everything," said Herr Grass. "Now we are prepared."

"Right," said the Sergeant irritably. "We'll go then. This bloody place is like an oven. My shirt's sticking to my back."

On the journey back, Herr Grass was more talkative. In slow, cautious English, he told them of his early childhood, of his work in the navy during the war, of his present job with the German War Graves Commission. The following day, he said, he and Herr Henreich would motor to County Clare and on the day after that, to County Galway. Then they would bring all the remains to the special cemetery in County Wicklow where there were already over fifty Germans buried. Then back to Berlin where Greta and his family of three boys were waiting for him. He showed them a photograph of Greta, a plump, carefree girl in shorts, by a lake.

Back in the police station, the Sergeant signed the

papers which stated that he had witnessed the exhumation and Burke signed as witness to the Sergeant's signature. Then Herr Grass and Herr Henreich added their names and left a duplicate copy of the papers with the Sergeant. They would not stay for a meal: they had to get back to Dublin that night. They thanked the two policemen for their assistance, apologized for taking up so much of their time and departed.

"They're gone," said Burke, looking after the car.

"Aye," said the Sergeant.

"It's no wonder they're a powerful nation; that's what I say. Did you ever see the beat of them for efficiency? And there they are away off with a dead man in the car with them and them as happy as lambs. What do you make of them, Sergeant? And did you see that second fella, the Herr Henry bucko, did you see him digging away there as if he was digging potatoes for the dinner? Never turned a hair on his head."

"Aye."

"And the other lad ticking off the names in his wee book like a grocer. Aw, but they're a powerful race of people. Powerful. And then when . . ."

"Aye, powerful," echoed the Sergeant, not knowing what he was saying. Then straightening his shoulders and pushing his stomach in with the flat of his hand, he said briskly, "Now, Burke, back inside with us to our own duties. Have you distributed those handbills about the dog licences?"

"This afternoon, Sergeant, I was going to do it."

"And the tillage census in the upper parish, have you finished it yet?"

"All but three or four houses, Sergeant. I'll do them in a while of an evening on the bicycle."

"Good," said the Sergeant. "That'll be that, then." The moment of efficiency died in him as quickly as it had begun. His shoulders slumped and his stomach crept out. "I don't know a damn what came over me out there," he said in a low voice, as if he were alone.

"What's that, Sergeant?"

"What in hell came over me? I never did the like of it in my life before. Never in all my years in the force. And then before foreigners too." He raised his cap inches above his head, slipped his fingers under it and fumbled with his scalp. He lowered the cap again. "I'm damned if I can understand it. The heat, maybe. The heat and the years . . . they're a treacherous combination, Burke, very treacherous."

"What are you talking about, Sergeant?" said Burke with exaggerated innocence.

"You know bloody well what I'm talking about. And I'll tell you something here and now, Burke." He prodded the guard's shoulder with his index finger. "If ever a word of what happened out there at Glennafuiseog breaks your lips, to any mortal man, now or ever, as God's my judge, Burke, I'll have you sent to the wildest outpost in the country. Now, get away out with you and distribute them handbills."

"Very good, Sergeant."

"And report to me again when you come back."

"Righto, Sergeant. Righto."

The Sergeant turned and waddled towards the building. For a man of his years and shape, he carried himself with considerable dignity.

The Mountains of Mourne

Gerry Adams

GEORDIE MAYNE LIVED in Urney Street, one of a net-
work of narrow streets which stretched from Cupar Street,
in the shadow of Clonard Monastery, to the Shankill
Road. I don't know where Geordie is now or even if he's
living or dead, but I think of him often. Though I knew
him only for a short time many years ago, Geordie is one
of those characters who might come into your life briefly
but never really leave you afterwards.

Urney Street is probably gone now. I haven't been there
in twenty years and all that side of the Shankill has disappeared since then as part of the redevelopment of the area.
Part of the infamous Peace Line follows the route that

GERRY ADAMS (1948–) was born in West Belfast, where
he resides with his wife and son. He was arrested and held without trial, for suspected IRA involvement, from 1973 to 1977. A
member of PEN, the international guild of writers, he has published numerous books including *Falls Memories* (1983), *The Politics of Irish Freedom* (1986), *A Pathway to Peace* (1988), *Cage
Eleven* (1990), *The Street and Other Stories* (1992), plus *Selected
Writings* (1994).

Cupar Street used to take. Before the Peace Line was erected Lawnbrook Avenue joined Cupar Street to the Shankill Road. Cupar Street used to run from the Falls Road up until it met Lawnbrook Avenue, then it swung left and ran on to the Springfield Road. Only as I try to place the old streets do I realize how much the place has changed this last twenty years, and how little distance there really is between the Falls and the Shankill. For all that closeness there might as well be a thousand miles between them.

When we were kids we used to take shortcuts up Cupar Street from the Falls to the Springfield Road. Catholics lived in the bottom end of Cupar Street nearest the Falls; there were one or two in the middle of Cupar Street, too, but the rest were mainly Protestants till you got up past Lawnbrook Avenue, and from there to the Springfield Road was all Catholic again. The streets going up the Springfield Road on the right-hand side were Protestant and the ones on the left-hand side up as far as the Flush were Catholic. After that both sides were nearly all Protestant until you got to Ballymurphy.

When we were kids we paid no heed to these territorial niceties, though once or twice during the Orange marching season we'd get chased. Around about the twelfth of July and at other appropriate dates the Orangemen marched through many of those streets, Catholic and Protestant alike. The Catholic ones got special attention, as did individual Catholic houses, with the marching bands and their followers, sometimes the worse for drink, exciting themselves with enthusiastic renderings of Orange tunes as they passed by. The Mackie's workers also passed that way twice daily, an especially large contingent making its way from the Shankill along Cupar Street to Mackie's Foundry. The largest engineering works in the city was surrounded by Catholic streets, but it employed very few Catholics.

Often bemused by expressions such as "Catholic street" and "Protestant area," I find myself nonetheless using the very same expressions. How could a house be Catholic or Protestant? Yet when it comes to writing about the reality it's hard to find other words. Though loath to do so, I use the terms "Catholic" and "Protestant" here to encompass the various elements who make up the unionist and non-unionist citizens of this state.

It wasn't my intention to tell you all this. I could write a book about the *craic* I had as a child making my way in and out of all those wee streets on the way back and forth to school or the Boys' Confraternity in Clonard or even down at the Springfield Road dam fishing for spricks, but that's not what I set out to tell you about. I set out to tell you about Geordie Mayne of Urney Street. Geordie was an Orangeman, nominally at least. He never talked about it to me except on the occasion when he told me that he was one. His lodge was The Pride of the Shankill Loyal Orange Lodge, I think, though it's hard to be sure after all this time.

I only knew Geordie for a couple of weeks, but even though that may seem too short a time to make a judgment I could never imagine him as a zealot or a bigot. You get so that you can tell, and by my reckoning Geordie wasn't the worst. He was a driver for a big drinks firm: that's how I met him. I was on the run at the time. It was almost

Christmas 1969 and I had been running about like a blue-assed fly since early summer. I hadn't worked since July, we weren't getting any money except a few bob every so often for smokes, so things were pretty rough. But it was an exciting time: I was only twenty-one and I was one of a dozen young men and women who were up to their necks in trying to sort things out.

To say that I was on the run is to exaggerate a little. I wasn't wanted for anything, but I wasn't taking any chances either. I hadn't slept at home since the end of May when the RUC had invaded Hooker Street in Ardoyne and there had been a night or two of sporadic rioting. Most of us who were politically active started to take precautions at that time. We were expecting internment or worse as the civil rights agitation and the reaction against it continued to escalate. Everything came to a head in August, including internment, and in Belfast the conflict had been particularly sharp around Cupar Street. This abated a little, but we thought it was only a temporary respite: with the British Army on the streets it couldn't be long till things hotted up again. In the meantime we were not making ourselves too available.

Conway Street, Cupar Street at the Falls Road end, and all of Norfolk Street had been completely burned out on the first night of the August pogrom; further up, near the monastery, Bombay Street was gutted on the following night. These were all Catholic streets. Urney Street was just a stone's throw from Bombay Street; that is, if you were a stone thrower.

The drinks company Geordie worked for were taking on extra help to cope with the Christmas rush, and a few of us went up to the head office on the Glen Road on spec one morning; as luck would have it I got a start, together with Big Eamonn and two others. I was told to report to the store down in Cullingtree Road the next morning and it was there that I met Geordie.

He saw me before I saw him. I was standing in the big yard among all the vans and lorries and I heard this voice shouting. "Joe . . . Joe Moody."

I paid no attention.

"Hi, boy! Is your name Joe Moody?" the voice repeated. With a start I realised that that was indeed my name, or at least it was the bum name I'd given when I'd applied for the job.

"Sorry," I stammered.

"I thought you were corned beef. C'mon over here."

I did as instructed and found myself beside a well-built, red-haired man in his late thirties. He was standing at the back of a large empty van.

"Let's go, our kid. My name's Geordie Mayne. We'll be working together. We're late. Have you clocked in? Do it over there and then let's get this thing loaded up."

He handed me a sheaf of dockets.

"Pack them in that order. Start from the back. I'll only be a minute."

He disappeared into the back of the store. I had hardly started to load the van when he arrived back. Between the two of us we weren't long packing in the cartons and crates of wines and spirits and then we were off, Geordie cheerfully saluting the men on barricade duty at the end of the street as they waved us out of the Falls area and into the rest of the world.

Geordie and I spent most of our first day together delivering our load to off-licenses and public houses in the city center. I was nervous of being recognized because I had worked in a bar there, but luckily it got its deliveries from a different firm. It was the first day I had been in the city center since August; except for the one trip to Dublin and one up to Derry I had spent all my time behind the barricades. It was disconcerting to find that, apart from the unusual sight of British soldiers with their cheerful, arrogant voices, life in the center of Belfast, or at least its licensed premises, appeared unaffected by the upheavals of the past few months. It was also strange as we made our deliveries to catch glimpses on television of news coverage about the very areas and issues I was so involved in and familiar with. Looked at from outside through the television screen, the familiar scenes might as well have been in another country.

Geordie and I said nothing of any of this to one another. That was a strange experience for me, too. My life had been so full of the cut-and-thrust of analysis, argument and counterargument about everything that affected the political situation that I found it difficult to restrain myself from commenting on events to this stranger. Indeed, emerging from the close camaraderie of my closed world, as I had done only that morning, I found it unusual even to be with a stranger. Over a lunch of soup and bread rolls in the Harp Bar in High Street I listened to the midday news on the BBC's Radio Ulster while all the time pretending indifference. The lead item was a story about an IRA convention and media speculation about a republican split. It would be nightfall before I would be able to check this out for myself, though a few times during the day I almost left Geordie in his world of cheerful pubs and publicans for the security of the ghettos.

The next few days followed a similar pattern. Each morning started with Geordie absenting himself for a few minutes to the back of the store while I started loading up the van. Then we were off from within the no-go areas and into the city center. By the end of the first week the two of us were like old friends. Our avoidance of political topics, even of the most pressing nature, that unspoken and much-used form of political protection and survival developed through expediency, had in its own way been a political indicator, a signal, that we came from "different sides."

In the middle of the second week Geordie broke our mutual and instinctive silence on this issue when with a laugh he handed me that morning's dockets. "Well, our kid, this is your lucky day. You're going to see how the other half lives. We're for the Shankill."

My obvious alarm fuelled his amusement.

"Oh, aye," he guffawed. "It's all right for me to traipse up and down the Falls every day, but my wee Fenian friend doesn't want to return the favor."

I was going to tell him that nobody from the Falls went up the Shankill burning down houses, but I didn't. I didn't want to hurt his feelings, but I didn't want to go up the Shankill either. I was in a quandary and set about loading up our deliveries with a heavy heart. After I had only two of the cartons loaded I went to the back of the store to tell Geordie that I was jacking it in. He was in the wee office with oul' Harry the storeman. Each of them had a glass of spirits in his hand. Geordie saw me coming and offered his to me.

"Here, our kid, it's best Jamaican rum. A bit of Dutch courage never did anyone any harm."

"Nawh thanks, Geordie, I don't drink spirits. I need to talk to you for a minute . . ."

"If it's about today's deliveries, you've nothing to worry about. We've only one delivery up the Shankill and don't be thinking of not going 'cos you'll end up out on your arse. It's company policy that mixed crews deliver all over the town. Isn't that right, Harry?"

Harry nodded in agreement.

"C'mon, our kid. I'll do the delivery for you. Okay? You can sit in the van. How's that grab you? Can't be fairer than that, can I, Harry?"

"Nope," Harry grunted. They drained their glasses.

"I'll take a few beers for the child, Harry," Geordie said over his shoulder as he and I walked back to the van.

"You know where they are," said Harry.

"Let's go," said Geordie to me. "It's not every day a wee Fenian like you gets on to the best road in Belfast . . ."— he grabbed me around the neck—". . . and off it again in one piece. Hahaha."

That's how I ended up on the Shankill. It wasn't so bad but before I tell you about that, in case I forget, from then on, each morning when Geordie returned from the back of the store after getting his "wee drop of starting fuel" he always had a few bottles of beer for me.

Anyway, back to the job in hand. As Geordie said, we only had the one order on the Shankill. It was to the Long Bar. We drove up by Unity Flats and on to Peter's Hill. There were no signs of barricades like the ones on the Falls, and apart from a patrolling RUC Land Rover and two British Army jeeps the road was the same as it had always seemed to me. Busy and prosperous and coming awake in the early winter morning sunshine.

A few months earlier, in October, the place had erupted in protest at the news that the B Specials were to be disbanded. The protesters had killed one RUC man and wounded three others; thirteen British soldiers had been injured. In a night of heavy gun fighting along the Shankill Road the British had killed two civilians and wounded twenty others. Since then there had been frequent protests here against the existence of no-go areas in Catholic parts of Belfast and Derry.

Mindful of all this, I perched uneasily in the front of the van, ready at a second's notice to spring into Geordie's seat and drive like the blazes back whence I came. I needn't have worried. Geordie was back in moments. As he climbed into the driver's seat he threw me a packet of cigarettes.

"There's your Christmas box, our kid. I told them I had a wee Fenian out here and that you were dying for a smoke."

Then he took me completely by surprise.

"Do y' fancy a fish supper? It's all right! We eat fish on Friday as well. Hold on!"

And before I could say anything he had left me again as he sprinted from the van into the Eagle Supper Saloon.

"I never got any breakfast," he explained on his return. "We'll go 'round to my house. There's nobody in."

I said nothing as we turned into Westmoreland Street and in through a myriad of backstreets till we arrived in Urney Street. Here the tension was palpable, for me at least. Geordie's house was no different from ours. A two-bedroomed house with a toilet in the backyard and a modernized scullery. Only for the picture of the British Queen, I could have been in my own street. I buttered rounds of plain white bread and we wolfed down our fish suppers with lashings of Geordie's tea.

Afterwards, my confidence restored slightly, while Geordie was turning the van in the narrow street I walked down to the corner and gazed along the desolation of Cupar Street up towards what remained of Bombay Street. A British soldier in a sandbagged emplacement greeted me in a John Lennon accent.

"'Lo, moite. How's about you?"

I ignored him and stood momentarily immersed in the bleak pitifulness of it all, from the charred remains of the small houses to where the world-weary slopes of Divis Mountain gazed benignly in their winter greenness down on us where we slunk, blighted, below the wise steeples of Clonard. It was Geordie's impatient honking of the horn that shook me out of my reverie. I nodded to the British soldier as I departed. This time he ignored me.

"Not a pretty sight," Geordie said as I climbed into the van beside him.

I said nothing. We made our way back through the side streets on to the Shankill again in silence. As we turned into Royal Avenue at the corner of North Street he turned to me.

"By the way," he said, "I wasn't there that night."

There was just a hint of an edge in his voice.

"I'm sorry! I'm not blaming you," I replied. "It's not your fault."

"I know," he told me firmly.

That weekend, subsidized by my week's wages, I was immersed once more in subversion. That at least was how the unionist government viewed the flurry of political activity in the ghettos, and indeed a similar view was taken by those representatives of the Catholic middle class who had belatedly attached themselves to the various committees in which some of us had long been active. On Monday I was back delivering drink.

We spent the week before Christmas in County Down, seemingly a million miles from the troubles and the tension of Belfast town. For the first time in years I did no political work. It was late by the time we got back each night and I was too tired, so that by Wednesday I realized that I hadn't even seen, read or heard any news all that week. I smiled to myself at the thought that both I and the struggle appeared to be surviving without each other; in those days that was a big admission for me to make, even to myself.

In its place Geordie and I spent the week up and down country roads, driving through beautiful landscapes, over and around hilltops and along rugged seashores and lough sides as we ferried our liquid wares from village to town, from town to port and back to village again; from market town to fishing village, from remote hamlet to busy crossroads. Even yet the names have a magical sound for me, and at each one Geordie and I took the time for a stroll or a quick look at some local antiquity.

One memorable day we journeyed out to Comber and from there to Killyleagh and Downpatrick, to Crossgar and back again and along the Ballyhornan road and on out to Strangford where we ate our cooked ham baps and

drank bottles of stout, hunkering down from the wind
below the square tower of Strangford Castle, half-frozen
with the cold as we looked over towards Portaferry on the
opposite side, at the edge of the Ards Peninsula. We spent
a day there as well, and by this time I had a guidebook with
me written by Richard Hayward, and I kept up a commentary as we toured the peninsula, from Millisle the
whole way around the coastline and back to Newtownards.
By the end of the week we had both seen where the Norse-
men had settled and the spot where Thomas Russell, "the
man from God knows where," was hanged, where Saint
Patrick had lived and Cromwell and Betsy Grey and Shane
O'Neill. We visited monastic settlements and stone circles,
round towers, dolmens and holy wells. Up and down the
basket-of-eggs county we walked old battle sites like those
of the faction fights at Dolly's Brae or Scarva, "wee buns"
we learned compared to Saintfield where Munroe and
7,000 United Irishmen routed the English forces, or the
unsuccessful three-year siege by the Great O'Neill, the
Earl of Tyrone, of Jordan's Castle at Ardglass. And in
between all this we delivered our cargoes of spirits and fine
wines.

This was a new world to me, and to Geordie too. It was
a marked contrast to the smoke and smell and claustro-
phobic closeness of our Belfast ghettos and the conflicting
moods which gripped them in that winter of 1969. Here
was the excitement of greenery and wildlife, of rushing
water, of a lightness and heady clearness in the atmosphere
and of strange magic around ancient pagan holy places. We
planned our last few days' runs as tours and loaded the van
accordingly so that whereas in the city we took the short-

est route, now we steered according to Richard Hayward's guidebook.

On Christmas Eve we went first to Newry where we unloaded over half our supplies in a series of drops at that town's licensed premises. By lunchtime we were ready for the run along the coast road to Newcastle, skirting the Mournes, and from there back home. At our last call on the way out to the Warrenpoint Road, the publican set us up two pints as a Christmas box. The pub was empty and as we sat there enjoying the sup a white-haired man in his late sixties came in. He was out of breath, weighed down with a box full of groceries.

"A bully, John," he greeted the publican. "Have I missed the bus?"

"Indeed and you have, Paddy, and he waited for you for as long as he could."

Paddy put his box down on the floor. His face was flushed.

"Well, God's curse on it anyway. I met Peadar Hartley and big MacCaughley up the town and the pair of them on the tear, and nothing would do them boys but we'd have a Christmas drink and then another till they put me off my whole way of going with their ceili-ing and oul' palavering. And now I've missed the bloody bus. God's curse on them two rogues. It'll be dark before there's another one."

He sighed resignedly and pulled a stool over to the bar, saluting the two of us as he did so.

"John, I might as well have a drink when I'm this far and give these two men one as well."

He overruled our protests.

"For the season that's in it. One more'll do yous no

harm. It's Christmas. Isn't that right, John? And one for yourself and I'll have a wee Black Bush meself."

"Will you have anything in the Bush, Paddy?"

"Indeed and I'll not. Now John, if it was Scotch now I'd have to have water or ginger ale or something but that's only with Scotch. I take nothing in my whiskey!"

We all joined him in his delighted laughter.

"What way are yous going, boys? Did you say yous were going out towards Newcastle?" the publican asked us.

Geordie nodded.

"Could you ever drop oul' Paddy out that road? He has to go as far as Kilkeel and by the looks of him if he doesn't go soon he'll be here till the New Year."

"No problem," Geordie grinned. I could see he was enjoying the old man who was now lilting merrily away to himself.

"De euw did eh euw, did eh euw did del de."

"Paddy, these two men'll give you a wee lift home."

Paddy was delighted.

"Surely to God, boys, but yous is great men so yous are. Here, we'll have another wee one before we go. A wee *deoch don dorais.* All right, John?"

"Indeed and it isn't," John told him. "Kate'll be worrying about you and these two lads can't wait. Isn't that right, boys?"

"Well, let it never be said that I kept men from their work," Paddy compromised.

"A happy New Year to you, John." The three of us saluted our host and retreated into the crisp afternoon air.

"It'll snow the night," our newfound friend and passenger announced, sniffing the air. I was carrying his box.

He did a jig, to Geordie's great amusement, when he saw that we were traveling in a drinks van.

"It'll be the talk of the place!" he laughed as we settled him into the passenger seat while I wedged myself against the door. Geordie gave him a bottle of stout as we pulled away.

"Do you want a glass?" I asked. "There's some here."

"A glass? Sure yous are well organized. Yous must be from Belfast! No, son, I don't need a glass, thanks all the same. This is grand by the neck. By the way, my name's Paddy O'Brien."

We introduced ourselves.

"You'll never get a job in the shipyard with a name like that," Geordie slagged him.

"And I wouldn't want it. 'Tis an Orange hole, begging your pardon lads and no offence, but them that's there neither works nor wants."

To my relief Geordie guffawed loudly, winking at me as he did. For the rest of the journey Paddy regaled us with stories of his mishaps in black holes and other places.

"I wouldn't like to live in Belfast. I'll tell yous that for sure. I worked there often enough, in both quarters mind you, and I always found the people as decent as people anywhere else. I was at the building and I went often enough to Casement Park, surely to God I did, for the football and some grand games I saw, but I wouldn't live there. Thon's a tough town!"

"It's not so bad," I said loyally, while all the time looking beyond Paddy and past Geordie to where Narrow Water flashed past us and the hills of County Louth dipped their toes in Carlingford Bay.

"No, give me the Mournes," Paddy persisted. "Were yous ever in the Mournes?" He emphasised "in."

"Nawh," we told him. Geordie began to enthuse about our week journeying around the county.

"Sure yous have a great time of it," Paddy agreed. "I'll come with yous the next time. Work? Yous wouldn't know what work was. But boys, I'm telling yous this. Don't be leaving this day without going into the Mournes. There's a road yous could take, wouldn't be out of your way, so it wouldn't. After yous drop me off, go on towards Annalong on this road, and a wee bit outside the village on the New-castle side there's a side road at Glassdrummond that'll take you up to Silent Valley. It's a straight road from here right through to Glassdrummond, boys. Yous can't miss it."

"That sounds good to me," Geordie agreed.

"Well, that's the best I can do for yous, boys. Come back some day and I'll take yous on better roads right into the heart of the mountains, but it'll be dark soon and snowing as well and my Kate'll kill me, so the Silent Valley'll have t' do yous. You'll be able to see where yous Belfast ones gets your good County Down water from to water your whiskey with and to wash your necks."

"Is Slieve Donard the highest of the Mournes?" I asked, trying to find my faithful guide book below Paddy's seat.

"Donard? The highest? It'll only take you a couple of hours to climb up there; but, boys, you could see the whole world from Slieve Donard. That's where Saint Donard had his cell, up on the summit. You'll see the Isle of Man out to the east and up along our own coast all of Strangford Lough and up to the hills of Belfast and the smoke rising above them, and beyond that on a clear day Lough Neagh and as far as Slieve Gallion on the Derry and Tyrone border. And southwards beyond Newry you'll see Slieve Gullion, where Cúchulainn rambled, and Slieve Foy east of there, behind Carlingford town, and farther south again you'll see the Hill of Howth and beyond that again if the day is good the Sugar Loaf and the Wicklow Mountains'll just be on the horizon."

"That's some view," Geordie said in disbelief.

Paddy hardly heard as he looked pensively ahead at the open road.

"There's only one thing you can't see from Donard, and many people can't see it anyway although it's the talk of the whole place, and even if it jumped up and bit you it's not to be seen from up there among all the sights. Do yous know what I'm getting at, boys? It's the cause of all our cursed troubles, and if you were twice as high as Donard you couldn't see it. Do yous know what it is?"

We both waited expectantly, I with a little trepidation, for him to enlighten us.

"The bloody border," he announced eventually. "You can't see that awful bloody imaginary line that they pretend can divide the air and the mountain ranges and the rivers, and all it really divides is the people. You can see everything from Donard, but isn't it funny you can't see that bloody border?"

I could see Geordie's hands tighten slightly on the steering-wheel. He continued smiling all the same.

"And there's something else," Paddy continued. "Listen to all the names: Slieve Donard, or Bearnagh or Meelbeg or Meelmore—all in our own language. For all their efforts they've never killed that either. Even most of the wee

Orange holes: what are they called? Irish names. From Bal-
lymena to Ahoghill to the Shankill, Aughrim, Derry and
the Boyne. The next time yous boys get talking to some of
them Belfast Orangemen you should tell them that."

"I'm a Belfast Orangeman," Geordie told him before I
could say a word. I nearly died, but Paddy laughed uproar-
iously. I said nothing. I could see that Geordie was starting to take the needle. We passed through Kilkeel with
only Paddy's chortling breaking the silence.

"You're the quare *craic*," he laughed. "I've really enjoyed
this wee trip. Yous are two decent men. *Tá mise go han
buíoch daoibh, a cháirde.* I'm very grateful to you indeed."

"*Tá fáilte romhat*," I said, glad in a way that we were near
his journey's end.

"Oh, *maith an fear*," he replied. "*Tabhair dom do lámh.*"
We shook hands.

"What d'fuck's yous two on about?" Geordie interrupted
angrily.

"He's only thanking us and I'm telling him he's welcome," I explained quickly. "Shake hands with him!"

Geordie did so grudgingly as the old man directed him
to stop by the side of the road.

"Happy Christmas," he proclaimed as he lifted his box.

"Happy Christmas," we told him. He stretched across
me and shook hands with Geordie again.

"*Go n'éirigh an bóthar libh*," he said. "May the road rise
before you."

"And you," I shouted, pulling closed the van door as
Geordie drove off quickly and Paddy and his box vanished
into the shadows.

"Why don't yous talk bloody English," Geordie snarled

savagely at me as he slammed through the gears and catapulted the van forward.

"He just wished you a safe journey," I said lamely. "He had too much to drink and he was only an old man. It is Christmas after all."

"That's right, you stick up for him. He wasn't slow about getting his wee digs in, Christmas or no Christmas. I need a real drink after all that oul' balls."

He pulled the van roughly into the verge again. I got out too as he clambered outside and climbed into the back. Angrily he selected a carton of whiskey from among its fellows and handed me a yellow bucket which was wedged in among the boxes.

"Here, hold this," he ordered gruffly. As I did so he held the whiskey box at arm's length above his head and then, to my surprise, dropped it on the road. We heard glass smashing and splintering as the carton crumpled at one corner. Geordie pulled the bucket from me and sat the corner of the whiskey box into it.

"Breakages," he grinned at my uneasiness. "You can't avoid them. By the time we get to Paddy's Silent bloody Valley there'll be a nice wee drink for us to toast him and the border *and* that bloody foreign language of yours. Take that in the front with you."

I did as he directed. Already the whiskey was beginning to drip into the bucket.

"That's an old trick," Geordie explained as we continued our journey. He was still in bad humor and maybe even a little embarrassed about the whiskey, which continued to dribble into the bucket between my feet on the floor. "The cardboard acts as a filter and stops any glass from getting through. Anyway, it's Christmas and Paddy isn't the only one who can enjoy himself," he concluded as we took the side road at Glassdrummond and commenced the climb up to the Silent Valley.

The view that awaited us was indeed breathtaking, as we came suddenly upon the deep mountain valley with its massive dam and huge expanse of water surrounded by rugged mountains and skirted by a picturesque stretch of road.

"Well, Paddy was right about this bit anyway," Geordie conceded as he parked the van and we got out for a better view. "It's a pity we didn't take a camera with us," he said. "It's gorgeous here. Give's the bucket and two of them glasses."

He filled the two glasses and handed me one.

"Don't mind me, our kid. I'm not at myself. Here's to a good Christmas."

That was the first time I drank whiskey. I didn't want to offend Geordie again by refusing but I might as well have for I put my foot in it anyway the next minute. He was gazing reflectively up the valley, quaffing his drink with relish while I sipped timorously on mine.

"Do you not think you're drinking too much to be driving?" I asked.

He exploded.

"Look son, I've stuck you for a few weeks now, and I never told you once how to conduct your affairs; not once. You've gabbled on at me all week about every bloody thing under the sun and today to make matters worse you and that oul' degenerate that I was stupid enough to give a lift to, you and him tried to coerce me and talked about me in your stupid language, and now you're complaining about my driving. When you started as my helper I didn't think I'd have to take the pledge *and* join the fuckin' rebels as well. Give my head peace, would you, wee lad; for the love and honor of God, give's a bloody break!"

His angry voice skimmed across the water and bounced back at us off the side of the mountains. I could feel the blood rushing to my own head as the whiskey and Geordie's words registered in my brain.

"Who the hell do you think you are, eh?" I shouted at him, and my voice clashed with the echo of his as they collided across the still waters.

"Who do I think I am? Who do you think you are is more like it," he snapped back, "with all your bright ideas about history and language and all that crap. You and that oul' eejit Paddy are pups from the same Fenian litter, but you remember one thing, young fella-me-lad, yous may have the music and songs and history and even the bloody mountains, but we've got everything else; you remember that!"

His outburst caught me by surprise.

"All that is yours as well, Geordie. We don't keep it from you. It's you that rejects it all. It doesn't reject you. It's not ours to give or take. You were born here same as me."

"I don't need you to tell me what's mine. I know what's mine. I know where I was born. You can keep all your emotional crap. Like I said, we've got all the rest."

"Who's 'we,' Geordie? Eh? Who's 'we'? The bloody English Queen or Lord bloody Terence O'Neill, or Chi-Chi, the dodo that's in charge now? Is that who 'we' is? You've got all the rest! Is that right, Geordie? That's shit and you know it."

I grabbed him by the arm and spun him round to face me. For a minute I thought he was going to hit me. I was ready for him. But he said nothing as we stood glaring at each other.

"You've got fuck all, Geordie," I told him. "Fuck all except a two-bedroomed house in Urney Street and an identity crisis."

He turned away from me and hurled his glass into the darkening distance.

"This'll nivver be Silent Valley again, not after we're finished with it," he laughed heavily. "I'm an Orangeman, Joe. That's what I am. It's what my Da was. I don't agree with everything here. My Da wouldn't even talk to a Papist, nivver mind drink or work with one, When I was listening to Paddy I could see why. That's what all this civil rights rubbish is about as well. Well, I don't mind people having their civil rights. That's fair enough. But you know and I know if it wasn't that it would be something else. I'm easy come, easy go. There'd be no trouble if everybody else was the same."

I had quietened down also by now.

"But people need their rights," I said.

"Amn't I only after saying that!" he challenged me.

"Well, what are you going to do about it?" I retorted.

"Me?" he laughed. "Now I know your head's cut! I'm going to do exactly nothing about it! There are a few things that make me different from you. We've a lot in common, I grant you that, but we're different also, and one of the differences is that after Christmas I'll have a job and you won't, and I intend to keep it. And more importantly, I intend to stay alive to do it."

"Well, that's straight enough and there's no answer to that," I mused, sipping the last of my whiskey.

Geordie laughed at me.

"Typical Fenian," he commented. "I notice you didn't throw away your drink."

"What we have we hold." I took another wee sip and gave him the last of it.

"By the way, seeing we're talking to each other instead of at each other, there's no way that our ones, and that includes me, will ever let Dublin rule us."

The sun was setting and there was a few wee flurries of snow in the air.

"Why not?" I asked.

"'Cos that's the way it is."

"What we have we hold?" I repeated. "Only for real."

"If you like."

"But you've nothing in common with the English. We don't need them here to rule us. We can do a better job ourselves. They don't care about the unionists. You go there and they treat you like a Paddy just like me. What do you do with all your loyalty then? You're Irish. Why not claim that and we'll all govern Dublin."

"I'm British!"

"So am I," I exclaimed. "Under duress 'cos I was born in this state. We're both British subjects but we're Irishmen. Who do you support in the rugby? Ireland I bet! Or international soccer? The same! All your instincts and roots and . . ."—I waved my arms around at the dusky mountains in frustration—". . . surroundings are Irish. This is fucking Ireland. It's County Down, not Sussex or Suffolk or Yorkshire. It's us and we're it!" I shouted.

"Now you're getting excited again. You shouldn't drink whiskey," Geordie teased me. "It's time we were going. C'mon; I surrender."

On the way down to Newcastle I drank the whiskey that was left in the bucket. We had only one call to make, so when I asked him to, Geordie dropped me at the beach. I stood watching as the van drove off and thought that perhaps he wouldn't return for me. It was dark by now. As I walked along the strand the snow started in earnest. Slieve Donard was but a hulking shadow behind me. I couldn't see it. Here I was in Newcastle, on the beach. On my own, in the dark. Drunk. On Christmas Eve. Waiting for a bloody Orangeman to come back for me so that I could go home.

The snow was lying momentarily on the sand, and the water rushing in to meet it looked strange in the moonlight as it and the sand and the snow merged. I was suddenly exhilarated by my involvement with all these elements and as I crunched the sand and snow beneath my feet and the flakes swirled around me my earlier frustrations disappeared. Then I chuckled aloud at the irony of it all.

The headlights of the van caught me in their glare. My Orangeman had returned.

"You're soaked, you bloody eejit," he complained when I climbed into the van again.

He, too, was in better form. As we drove home it was as if we had never had a row. We had a sing-song—mostly carols with some Beatles' numbers—and the both of us stayed well clear of any contentious verses. On the way through the Belfast suburbs Geordie sang what we called "our song."

O Mary, this London's a wonderful sight
There's people here working by day and by night:
They don't grow potatoes or barley or wheat,
But there's gangs of them digging for gold in the street.
At least when I asked them that's what I was told,
So I took a hand at this digging for gold,
For all that I found there I might as well be
Where the Mountains of Mourne sweep down to the sea.

We went in for a last drink after we'd clocked out at the store, but by this time my head was thumping and I just wanted to go home.

As we walked back to the van Geordie shook my hand warmly.

"Thanks, kid. I've learned a lot this last week or so, and not just about County Down. You're dead on, son," he smiled, "for a Fenian. Good luck to you anyway, oul' hand, in all that you do, but just remember, our kid, I love this place as much as you do."

"I know," I said. "I learned that much at least."

He dropped me off at Divis Street and drove off waving, on across the Falls towards the Shankill. I walked up to the Falls. That was the last I saw of Geordie Mayne. I hope he has survived the last twenty years and that he'll survive the next twenty as well. I hope we'll meet again in better times. He wasn't such a bad fella, for an Orangeman.

A Visit to Dublin

Patrick Kavanagh

FOR A LONG TIME I had been imagining that literary people would be interesting to meet. I wanted to meet A. E. and any other of the Dublin writers with whom I might be able to connect. But greater than my desire to meet the exalted beings of Literature was the road-hunger in my heart that cried out for dusty romance. I had listened to the journeymen shoemakers, common tramps, and uncommon tinkers. I had read Jim Tully and Patrick

PATRICK KAVANAGH (1904–1967) was born in Inniskeen, County Monaghan. His poetry collections include *The Great Hunger* (1942), *A Soul for Sale* (1947), *Recent Poems* (1958), *Come Dance with Kitty Stobling* (1960), *Collected Poems* (1964), and *Complete Poems of Patrick Kavanagh* (1972). He also published two novels: *The Green Fool* (1938) and *Tarry Flynn* (1948). Prose pieces include *Self Portrait* (1963), *November Haggard* (1971), and *Kavanagh's Weekly*, a facsimile of the paper published by Patrick and Peter Kavanagh in 1952. There is a statue of Kavanagh by Dublin's Grand Canal, inspired by his poem "Lines Written on a Seat on the Grand Canal, Dublin"—*O commemorate me where there is water, / Canal water preferably, so stilly / Greeny at the heart of summer. Brother / Commemorate me thus beautifully.*

Magill. The blood of tramps was in my veins: my father's father had come from the West; he had taken the road Queen Maeve took when that cattle-fancier was on the chase of the Brown Bull of Cooley.

On the ninetenth of December, 1931, I said to my mother:

"I'm going a bit of a journey."

"Musha where?" she asked in surprise.

"As far as Dublin," I said.

She thought I was mad.

"What nonsense are ye up to now? 'Twould fit ye better to be cleanin' the drain in the meadow and not have the flood drive us out of the place."

I was aware of the condition of the drain which was making a lake of our meadow.

"I'm walking to Dublin," I said, "and I don't care if the flood in the meadow rises high as the flood that floated Noah above Ararat."

She took it in good part and gave me all the change was in the house. My brother was privy to my adventure—he was fifteen years old then—and gave me good practical advice. I had in my pocket exactly three shillings and fourpence ha'penny.

I wore my working clothes and boots. On my trousers were the tramp-necessary rectangular knee patches, my jacket was down to beggar standard, my boots were a hobnailed pair of my own making. I made a great mistake in not taking a second pair of socks, or at least one clean pair.

I was off. I was going down the road of my dreams. I had intended keeping a diary of my journey, but after a few entries gave it up.

It was a beautiful morning, bright and crisp, one could almost imagine spring in the air. Spring was in my imagination at any rate. I remembered how the women used to call after us on our way to Carrick fair: "God be with ye on the Dublin road where nobody ever had luck." I walked at a brisk pace for the first five or six miles. I knew this part of the road too well and the road and its people knew me. I wanted as quickly as possible to get on to the strange roads where Romance wearing gold earrings was waiting for me.

"Good mornin'," a man near home saluted. "Where are ye bound for?" he inquired.

"A little bit of a journey," I said.

Ten miles from home I was in a strange country, among folk who wouldn't know me. I decided that it was time to test my skill as a beggar. I looked about me and selected a snug, well-kept house a few perches off the main road. It was a whitewashed thatched cottage. An ideal house, I said to myself. I never imagined it could be so difficult to break into the beggar trade. For half an hour I stood on the road trying to screw up my courage to the sticking place. I walked up the laneway to the house and turned back again. I was finding it very difficult to get rid of my peasant-solid pride.

I went to the door at last and leaning over the half-door muttered something. A woman came. She was a nice woman of about thirty years and turned out to be one of those creatures of whom tramps dream but never encounter. Spiritually and physically she was tender as a sheltered leaf.

"I want a sup of a drink," I said.

"Come inside," she invited.

It wouldn't require a great detective to guess that this was a young woman married to an old man. I was never a cold-blooded lover of the brazen images set up by poets in the name of Woman. But adultery is not for tramps: it is a respectable, well-fed sin.

As I entered, the kettle on the hob broke into a sweet song.

She set a chair for me near the fire and rinsed the teapot. I love the music the lid of a teapot makes.

"A sup of tay will do ye no harm," she said.

"You're too dacent," I said.

I told her a tale of glamorous grief. I said I hadn't tasted a morsel of food for the past twenty-four hours and that I had walked from Newry.

"Me poor fella," she murmured, three short words more eloquent than a bookful of godly sermons. I was an impostor. She put before me a blue mugful of strong tea, four thick slices of brown bread well buttered, and to crown it all a pair of duck eggs. I should have wished to stay a longer while in that house but I was a tramp and must travel on.

My feet were feeling a bit tender, though I had only gone ten miles. A granite milestone along the way told me it was forty-five miles to Dublin: the chiselled letter-grooves were filled with moss and I had to trace the letters with my finger like a blind man reading braille. These were the miles that were made in old gods' time when good measure was in fashion.

My belly was full but my starved soul had still to break its fast. I touched a kind-faced gentleman who was standing outside his fine house: I touched him for money. He whistled and not a pleasant tune—he was calling the dog. I didn't look back, like Lot's wife.

Just not to deliver judgment on fine-housed gentlemen I went up to another hall door that had a chromium-plated knocker. A low-set woman answered my knock; when I saw the face that was on her I knew she was a torturer of tramps.

"Give me a couple of coppers," I said. The slamming of that massive hall door generated an electrical current about my eyes. As I walked down the steps from that hall door I pronounced my final judgment on all well-housed people.

"A bad lot."

The evening was thickening about the view, and I had so far not added to my three and fourpence halfpenny.

I entered a blacksmith's forge. The smith, a big, round-shouldered man with a neck of red folding fat, was making shoes for hunters. I talked him to generosity. He was surprised when he heard I was on the road.

"Be the mortal day you could very nearly be a schoolmaster," he said. He searched in his trousers pockets and I imagined that I heard the sweet tinkle of silver. Then he went to his coat that hung on the vise and searched again.

I'm sorry," he said, "but that's all I've on me, twopence."

I took it and thanked him. As I moved off I overheard him say to himself: "He's not right wise, he doesn't look all there."

It was quite dark now. I was traveling through grassland, "Meath of the pastures," and the small houses I wanted were few and far between. I came up with a young man who had been seeing his girl. He was as decent and generous as men in love are. He gave me sixpence and after we parted he called after me.

"Wait, there's a few fags in this packet you might like."

Six cigarettes. I sat down on a bank of darkness and had my first smoke of the day. The smell of bacon and eggs being fried came to my hunger-acute nostrils. I followed my nose and called at the door whence came the smell. "We can't accommodate you," was the answer I got.

"I don't want accommodation," I said. "It's a meal I'm asking."

"We can't accommodate you."

Not far from this house was a smaller one. I pushed open the door. An old, half-blind woman was sitting by the hob all alone.

"What d'ye want?" she squealed.

"A bite to eat, woman, if you can spare it."

She hobbled over to the dresser and from the cupboard extracted a crust of white bread which would have attracted the attention of an archaeologist. She gave me the museum-piece and I walked out. I had scarcely swung my coattail free of her door when she most ungraciously, and with a loud click, turned the key in the lock.

I was wondering if I'd have to be content with a soldier's supper, when prosperous goodness appeared like a new star in the December sky.

I spoke to a young boy who was standing outside his gate listening with cocked ear. I told him how it was with me.

"My father and mother is in the fair," he told me, "and the divil a one is in the house but meself."

I went in, and between the young boy and myself we

produced an excellent supper. The clock standing in the back window said it was ten o'clock.

"Give no heed to that oul' clock," the boy warned me, "it never toul' the truth in its life."

The rattle of a cart reached our ears.

"That's thim," the lad said.

I left. I passed through Slane, the place I had often seen from the hills of my childhood. There were numerous haybarns here. By the light of matches I groped my way round one; it was filled to the top and I had to climb up a twenty-foot standard to bed.

I didn't sleep well. Between midnight and two o'clock a shiver ran through me. Bury myself as I did in blankets of sweet-smelling hay, I couldn't get warm. I was up early. When I put my hand in my pocket I had no money—lost in the bedclothes! I tossed the hay back, and my luck was in—I found all the money save the halfpenny. No doubt it had gone to seek its comrade in the till of some ladies' draper.

Here and there curly columns of smoke were rising from big chimneys. I got an excuse for a breakfast in a laborer's cottage—dry bread and weak tea. The woman of the house kept saying: "God help ye, me poor fella, or anybody has no home."

The weather was perfect, like a May day. I washed my face at a roadside pump. I wrote in my diary.

"Am now twenty miles from Dublin, left foot very sore, can get everything but money. Have just talked to two children going to school, a boy and girl. Cromwell was their name."

I broke a branch from an ash tree and made of it a walking stick. I passed through Ashbourne village at eleven o'clock. A crowd were gathering to see the meet of the Meath Hounds. I build these facts from another entry in my diary.

I gave up begging for money, it was a hopeless quest. I got tea in another cottage. The woman there had a twinkle in her eye.

"Yer not a tramp," she said.

"To my grief I am," I replied.

"Yer up to some cod-actin'," she declared. "I'd know a real tramp."

I put two slices of bread in my pocket, disregarding the rule in my native place: "Eat your fill and pocket none."

Nothing of importance happened to me between Ashbourne and Dublin. The road was giving me very bad value.

I arrived in the city at half past two. I was more helpless than a bull in a mist. Tramps should keep clear of all cities and Dublin in particular. The Dublin police are the scourge of tramps—worse than blisters. I kept fairly free from their strong grip and inquisitive tongues. I went to the National Library, as I was quite sure that the people there would know the whereabouts of every literary man and woman. I was mistaken.

"Where does A. E. hang out?" I asked. They didn't know, though they tried to give the impression that they did. They knew where he used to live—in Plunket House.

"Sure I know that myself," I told the fellow with the goatee beard who stood behind the counter. I called the office table the counter when speaking to them and that made them laugh.

"Maybe you could give me the address of some other poet," I said.

A woman searched in a book and after a long time extracted one address, that of Oliver St John Gogarty.

"Is that the best you can do?" I queried. And that was the best they could do.

When I was in the library I thought I could take advantage of the fact and get a book to read. Eliot's *The Waste Land* was being talked about at that time. I asked for *The Waste Land*. The man with the goatee beard wanted to know if it was a book on drainage, and before I could explain was almost on his way to procure one of that type for me. I should have said that I asked specifically for *The Waste Land* by T. S. Eliot, so that left the joke a far finer one.

I turned for Gogarty's house in Ely Place. Near the National Gallery I inquired my way of a man who was speaking Gaelic to a boy, evidently his son. The man was the Minister for Finance in the Free State. I knew him by eyesight as he was the Member for my own county. Close on the Minister's heels was a detective with whom I chatted when I had parted with the keeper of the State purse.

I mistook Gogarty's white-robed maid for his wife—or his mistress. I expected every poet to have a spare wife.

"Are you a patient?" she asked.

"Devil a that," I said.

She didn't understand my language but understood my clothes.

"I want to see the poet."

"Well, wait till I see if the Doctor is in."

She turned her back and as soon as she did I turned and ran up Ely Place with the sidelong gait of a thief.

I tried Plunket House. I knocked and a girl down under spoke to me. "Who are you looking for?"

"A. E.," I said.

She knew his address.

"You're a topper," I said. "You know more than the chaps in the National Library."

A. E. opened the door to me, and not merely the door of wood on his house in Rathgar. I was afraid of that man. He looked like a man who had awakened from a dark trance. His eyes stared at me like two nightmare eyes from which there was no escape. He appeared quite certain that I was a beggar. I regretted not having a fiddle under my arm to add a touch of wild color to my drab tramp.

When I had explained who I was he gave me a handshake as warm as I've ever got. I sat on a chair that was too comfortable. I wasn't used to easy chairs. If I had been traveling respectable I shouldn't have minded so much. My hobnailed boots as I watched them grew bigger and bigger. The patches on the knees of my trousers, because I sat on a low seat, stood up like two pictures on exhibition. I cursed, inwardly, those boots and those dark patches. I was partly aware, too, that my shinbones were visible.

A. E. started to talk in a voice that was musical as evening over ploughed fields. He talked while I interjected an odd word for decency's sake. He told me all his stock tales and pet philosophies. I was bored and tried, like the hypocrite I was, to affect deep embarrassment in the presence of genius. I wasn't listening to A. E. I was worried over the poor impression I was making. I was hungry—for poetry? Yes, but I was also physically hungry, and an empty stomach is a great egoist, and a bad listener to anything save the fizz of rashers on a pan.

I was a peasant and a peasant is a narrow surveyor of generous hearts.

He read me Whitman, of whom he was very fond, and also Emerson.

I didn't like Whitman and said so. I always thought him a writer who tried to bully his way to prophecy. Of Emerson at the time I had no opinions to offer. I found him out later to be a sugary humbug. His transcendental bunkum sickened me.

When A. E. told me how sorry he was that his girl was out I was shocked. Satisfaction for my appetite in a café would shatter my capital on the reef of bankruptcy.

He plopped to the floor and searched among the lower shelves for books. He kept picking out volumes till my eye was full. I didn't judge those books by their covers or by their contents, but by their weight. They would weigh four stones if they weighed an ounce. Emerson's works and Whitman's were in the pile as a matter of course. Victor Hugo was represented by his masterpiece *Les Misérables.* The emotional warmth of Hugo appealed to me. There was a book by a modern Syrian prophet which for many years helped me to prattle glib lies that looked like truth. George Moore's *Confessions of a Young Man,* the only book of that author I could ever stomach. There were two books by Dostoyevsky, *The Brothers Karamazov* and *The Idiot.* These two books were worth more than all the rest together. I read *The Idiot* twenty times at least. Of the books of verse I got two volumes by A. E. himself. A. E. wrote some poems that I like, even now in maturity. I got James Stephens collected in a beautiful binding. I read Stephens for a short while and tossed him aside for ever. I daren't read him as I would find myself imitating his beautiful rhythms. Stephens was one of my favorites and I had to ban him. I got a good anthology compiled by a Japanese professor, Mahata Sargu. The printer's errors in this book were beyond counting and often made hash of a lovely poem.

I put the books on my back and left. A. E. I didn't call on any other poets or writers on that day.

Night was in the city when I left A. E. with my load of literature.

I moped around Nelson's Pillar. The newsboys and hard cases talked very intimately to me. I was one of themselves. I was looking for a cheap lodging-house. One fellow suggested a St Vincent de Paul night shelter.

"Chroist, don't go there," another advised me, "they'd make ye pray there."

To one of the worst slum lodging houses in Gloucester Street I was directed. I paid sixpence for my bed. There were six other beds in the room which was at the top of a three-storied house. The stink of that room and those beds has never left my nostrils. My roommates were the derelicts of humanity. There was a blind man, a lame man, a horrible looking young fellow with no nose, only two little holes under his eyes, there was a deaf but not dumb man, and another with a look of the criminal. The communal sanitary convenience was a rusty bucket which hadn't been emptied from the night before, and had apparently never been scrubbed: it had a scum of many layers.

I laid my books beside me covered with the ragged quilt.

The next day was a fast day. I went to a café and—

taking a dispensation from the fast—ordered a breakfast of rashers and eggs. I had a long journey ahead of me and I knew that a man travels on his breakfast. As soon as I got clear of Dublin I sat down on the roadside and opened one of my books, *The Ring and the Book*. I couldn't read Browning. A motorcar passed by and a curiously amused face peeped out the back window. A girl from our country who recognized me. I was upset for she was a nice girl.

Forward again. People who saw me took me for a purveyor of heretical Bibles and shook their heads. A priest mounted on a beautiful bay horse pulled up and was all edge to know what kind were the books. He was interested in books, but not in Russian writers.

"Books by the great Russians," I told him I carried. The name of Russians was associated with barbarism and grizzly bears.

"Books by Russians?" he said. "That's strange." He trotted his horse off and I continued my journey north.

The only entry in my diary relating to my homeward journey was written here. This is the entry:

"Have just overheard two men talking about me. One of them said to the other: 'I wonder who yon kinat with the load of books would be?' The other answered: "Some lazy Rodney, I suppose, that wouldn't do a tap of honest work."

My journey home was a two-day misery. It was pouring rain as I crossed the Hill of Mullacrew. I passed safely through the village of Louth where the fairies had led myself and my mother astray. I was home.

Although I had seen A. E., had got books, and had tasted the road, I have always regretted going to Dublin. I had lost something which I could never regain from books.

I got to know Dublin much better later on. It is a city overrun by patrons of poetry and art who praise the poets and secure the jobs for their own relations. A Government—since—to whom poet, prophet, and imbecile are fellows with votes.

With the death of A. E. the only true friend of the Irish poets had passed. His genius was his generosity and—whether born of vanity as some say it was—it was practical, and not the soft-mouthed admiration that A. E.'s critics were in the habit of bestowing.

One of the best of the young Irish poets, F. R. Higgins, once told me that there was, he believed, more dishonesty in the literary city of Dublin than in any other quarter of the globe. Shelley said that poets were the legislators of the world. Dublin must have changed a lot since Shelley knew it.

Irish writers leave Ireland because sentimental praise, or hysterical pietarian dispraise, is no use in the mouth of a hungry man.

Permissions

Hugo Hamilton's "The Homesick Industry" from *The Faber Book of Best New Irish Stories*, edited by David Marcus. © 2005 Hugo Hamilton. Reprinted with the permission of the author.

Éilís Ní Dhuibhne's "A Visit to Newgrange" from *Midwife to the Fairies: New and Selected Stories* was published by Cork University Press/Attic Press. © 2001 Éilís Ní Dhuibhne by permission of Attic Press Ltd, Youngline Industrial Estate, Togher, Cork, Ireland.

Frank O'Connor's "The American Wife" originally appeared in *The Collected Stories of Frank O'Connor*, © 1981 by Harriet O'Donovan Sheehy, executrix of the estate of Frank O'Connor. Used by permission of Alfred A. Knopf, a division of Random House, Inc. Used by permission of Lyons & Pande International LLC for Canada and United Kingdom.

Seán Mac Mathúna's "The Man Who Stepped on His Soul" from *The Atheist and Other Stories* was published by Wolfhound Press. © 1987 Seán Mac Mathúna. Reprinted by permission of Seán Mac Mathúna.

Edna O'Brien's "A Scandalous Woman" from *A Frantic Heart: Selected Stories of Edna O'Brien* (London: Weidenfeld & Nicolson). © 1984 by Edna O'Brien. Reprinted with permission of Farrar, Straus & Giroux, LLC and International Creative Management, Inc.

Desmond Hogan's "The Last Time" from *A Link with the River*. © 1989 by Desmond Hogan. Reprinted with the permission of Farrar, Straus & Giroux, LLC and International Creative Management, Inc.

About the Editor

James Mc Elroy teaches at the University of California, Davis. His articles and reviews have appeared in *The New York Times, The Los Angeles Times,* and *The Irish Literary Supplement.* Forthcoming books include *Derek Mahon: A Study in Protestantism* (Belfast: Lagan Press) and *James Joyce: Ecological Perspectives* (New York: Edwin Mellen Press).